DANCING BACKWARD: AN ADVENTURE IN MALE SUBMISSION

Thomas Lavalle

Juno Unlimited

ISBN: 9781793889249

Cover design: Jun Ares / Cover image: © Dreamstime

This is an adult erotic novel that explores and emphasizes some
psychological aspects of female domination and male submission in a
committed, consensual relationship. However, the story does contain
descriptions of some fairly graphic scenes of "femdom" activities that
could be pigeonholed under the heading of "B&D," i.e., "bondage and
discipline." Readers under eighteen, and any who might find such
material offensive, should avoid these pages.

Also by the author:
Dancing Backward 2: Final Descent Into Male Submission
Dancing Backward 3: A Beloved Slave Reclaimed
Rapture and Capture: Three Tales of Irresistible Modern Goddesses
The author welcomes questions and comments on his blog:
thomaslavalle.blogspot.com
Or email: *thomaslavalle@gmail.com*

CONTENTS

EPIGRAPH

"The moral of the tale is this: whoever allows himself to be whipped, deserves to be whipped."
—Leopold Von Sacher-Masoch, *Venus In Furs*

CHAPTER ONE ~ BAD TIMING

The sales trip had been successful, but Kelly's flight home had been twice delayed, depositing her at the deserted airport at nearly three a.m. A further annoyance—her supposedly devoted househusband, Chris, wasn't on hand to pick her up. He'd apparently fallen asleep after the first delay; and now, according to his last apologetic text, wouldn't arrive for another twenty minutes. As a final indignity, after all Kelly's fellow passengers had yanked their bags off the carousel and headed out the exit doors, her big wheelie still hadn't made its appearance. Which was why she was standing at this lost-luggage counter, a beautiful blonde woman in a thoroughly foul mood, waiting for the drowsy night attendant to report back.

Damn Chris! How dare he inconvenience her like this—and worse, far worse, leave her alone and vulnerable in this godforsaken place at this time of night! Kelly scanned a nearby bank of security monitors, hoping to glimpse an airport cop or even a janitor with a floor buffer. But the only signs of life were an old guy in an overcoat slumped on a bench and a crewcut young man squatting amid a cluster of tapestry luggage. *He* might do in a crisis, Kelly decided. A polo shirt revealed muscled arms, and the squatting thighs looked powerful. But what was muscleboy doing with all that feminine luggage?

As if in answer to her question, a woman in a skirt suit came striding across an adjacent monitor. She was older than the guy by a decade or two, but regal looking in a bosomy way—nearly as well endowed as Kelly herself—with a glossy mane of dark hair and an

1

unmistakable air of command in her high-heeled stride. The tick-tock stiletto beat could be heard now, echoing through the baggage hall. Was that her cougar boy or trophy husband?

Kelly watched now with a spark of erotic speculation as the executive-looking woman exited one screen and reappeared on the next one over, approaching the squatting young man from behind. He had to hear her, but he kept his head down, rummaging in a zipper compartment, as if desperate to find something before his lady returned.

What happened next was totally unexpected. The woman came straight up behind the squatting man and kicked him hard, right in his cute bluejeaned ass. The pointed toe of her ankle-strap pump launched him forward in a facedown heap, toppling the tapestry luggage all around him.

Kelly gasped as if *she* had just been kicked. But the woman on-screen seemed completely unaffected by what she'd done. Kelly watched her bend over the sprawling figure and casually retrieve a scarf from his outflung hand. Straightening up, she knotted and tugged the scarf into place, then, with a toss of her dark mane, walked away without a backward glance. Leaving the young man to scramble up, shoulder two carry-ons, yank the handles of two big rolling bags, and hurry off in frantic pursuit.

Kelly continued to stare at the now-blank screen, trying to come to grips with what she'd witnessed.

"This your bag, Ma'am?" The attendant was back, towing her big wheelie with its purple yarn tied to the handle. "Got sent to the wrong carousel, Ma'am. It happens."

She snapped out of her trance. "Yes, that's it, thank you so much." From her purse Kelly dug out a ten dollar bill, which promptly vanished as he pushed a clipboard toward her.

"Sign here, if you don't mind, Ma'am."

A few moments later Kelly was outside, her blonde pixie coif feathering in the night breeze. The curb was empty, the street likewise, except for some distant taillights. The intriguing couple had clearly made a fast getaway. Too bad! She would have liked a better look at them. She relied on her imagination instead, picturing the woman reclining in the back of a luxury sedan with her Hitachi Magic Wand, her young man up front behind the wheel, buns aflame from her perfectly placed soccer kick.

Would he be sporting a chauffeur's cap? Kelly thought not, but another detail did appear in her conjuring. Fastened around his muscular neck was a black leather collar.

Was that kinky little accessory also a product of Kelly's imagination? But no! She'd definitely seen it. In fact, she could see it now in vivid memory on that black-and-white surveillance screen. Muscleboy had worn a dog collar exactly like that.

Which meant he wasn't just cougar meat or trophy husband. *He was the dark-haired woman's real-life collared slave.*

Once again Kelly scanned the sidewalk. Verifying that she was quite alone, she slipped a hand down the front of her short, batik skirt and inside her panty front, letting her fingertips find and explore the sudden moistness between her thighs.

Dear God! That sordid little scene had not only turned her into a shameless voyeur, but actually excited her! And yet… hadn't she been shocked and deeply offended by the older woman's careless cruelty? And repelled by the younger man's cringing acceptance? Imagine, letting a woman treat him like a dog!

Yes, Kelly had felt all those things, and properly so. But that wasn't *all* she had felt. Because she wasn't just a bit moist down there, she was seriously wet.

Of course, she knew why. Kelly Ann Sheffield had been "born bossy," as her father liked to brag. It was a feature regularly noted by her teachers and playmates, and her natural bossiness remained an undeniable asset in her success as an aggressive saleswoman. Knowing that about herself, Kelly always went out of her way to treat her friends and colleagues, and certainly her customers, with great courtesy and kindness. She rarely barked at waiters, even when service was substandard; she always tipped generously, wrote checks to a half-dozen charities.

Even in her romantic relationship with Chris, who from the very first had accepted her superior status, her leadership style was relaxed and affectionate. Seldom did Kelly find it necessary to take a peremptory tone with him, or to restrict his many privileges and freedoms. Even lately, as his lapses and shortcomings as a househusband were becoming harder to overlook, she continued to be tolerant and forgiving.

Yes, Kelly did believe males were inferior, but the idea of booting Christopher in the ass—as the dark-haired woman had done to her boy-toy—well, it was unthinkable. Frankly, Kelly couldn't remember the last time she'd had to slap Chris in earnest.

"Do you dominate him?" The question, in various forms, had been asked her dozens of times, usually by girlfriends envious of the way Chris catered to her, even back when they started dating, before she'd married him and made him her househusband.

Kelly would respond with something like, "If you mean with whips and handcuffs, no, sorry to disappoint you, but we're not into kink. Chris is my subordinate and, yes, he's submissive to me in many ways. He damned well better be! But he's not a masochist, and I'm certainly no sadist."

And that had been the truth, at least until five minutes ago. Now, after what she'd just seen and the primal feelings it had stirred deep within her, Kelly was not so sure. It was one thing to be turned off by hokey and distasteful femdom porn clips, like several she'd come across on the 'net, or all the copycat kink that had gone mainstream, like rock divas prancing and posing while domming their chorus boys.

But what she'd witnessed on that little screen just now had been real, not staged. She'd peeked through a kind of keyhole at an intimate, consensual relationship that celebrated the total empowerment of the female over the male—and the erotic appeal of that had shocked her.

Yet there was another aspect of the hot little scene that was nagging at her. The older woman's arrogant cruelty had gotten results—instant obedience from her well-tamed male. While Kelly's carefully cultivated tolerance of Chris' shortcomings had produced exactly what? Even more lapses in his performance, less attentiveness to her needs. The upshot was that Cougar Domme was now being chauffeured home while Kelly was still stuck here on the sidewalk, fuming.

As if cued by her thoughts, down to her left she spotted the familiar bi-xenon headlamps of her new Audi A8, swinging out from behind an airport van and moving into the curb lane.

Chris had arrived—finally! And yet, Kelly wasn't ready just now to deal properly with his transgressions. Her thoughts and emotions were in too much turmoil, and her anger was too raw. She needed time to calm herself and weigh the various courses of action, some of them quite drastic and far-reaching in their possible consequences, before making up her mind.

But all uncertainties aside, one thing was for sure. Their relationship was in for some very big changes.

*

As he drove his beautiful wife away from the airport, Chris wished she had vented at him, even a little. He'd sensed her barely suppressed anger when he'd pulled to the curb and leaped out to embrace her. Why else would she have sidestepped him and pointed disdainfully at her bags, as if he might actually forget to load them?

Then, as he'd hurried to open the passenger door, she'd shaken her head and pointed again, this time at the rear door. It had taken Chris a confused moment to realize that Kelly actually intended to ride *behind* him on the way home. "It's late, Christopher, and I'm terribly tired," was the explanation she'd offered as he handed her into the back seat. "We'll talk later."

He'd driven away a bit troubled—by the not-so-subtle rebuff and that "talk later" remark with its faintly ominous undertone. Every time Kelly went on one of these extended sales trips, Chris worried. She'd told him once, by way of reassurance, that she had a hard-and-fast rule against mixing sex with business, but she'd also admitted that looking sexy was an invaluable asset in dealing with her high-powered executive clientele, most of whom were of the decidedly male persuasion.

Of course, there wasn't a damn thing Chris could do about that. Simply put, Kelly Ann Sheffield could have any man she wanted, and Chris had pretty much learned to accept that and not ask questions. And, after a few miles, he'd managed to wall off most of his anxieties and insecurities and conjure up a brand-new fantasy in which he was chauffeuring around a fabulous film star. Kelly was certainly gorgeous enough for the part, lounging back there with her eyes shut, princess-perfect head tipped back, white-blond hair artfully askew.

How he had missed her! Which made it all the more unforgivable that he'd fallen asleep watching that basketball game, only to be jolted into wide-eyed panic hours later by her text message:

Just landed, sweetie, better get your ass here fast!

If Kelly only knew, there was a lot more than just tonight's failure to account for. During the ten days she'd been gone, calling on her top corporate accounts in the eleven Western states, Chris had basically screwed around—ordering pizza, renting action movies, binge-watching sports, even checking out a few online porn sites.

Only this morning—on the final day!—had he'd gone into panic mode and attacked his chore list, cleaning the kitchen and bathrooms, sweeping, mopping and vacuuming, ironing a half-dozen of Kelly's favorite skirts and blouses, throwing out all the pizza boxes and doing a frenzied last-minute shopping.

No wonder he'd nodded off during the game! He was exhausted!

But, much as he deserved a royal tongue-lashing for tonight's fuckup, not to mention the many previous lapses, Chris wasn't overly worried. The condo had looked pretty damned good on final inspection, if he did say so himself; and, anyway, she clearly wasn't going to scold him when they got home. Tomorrow, after a good night's sleep, she'd wake up in high spirits with her bubbly personality fully restored and forget all about that vague threat to "talk later." He could picture her in the breakfast nook, loosely wrapped in that sexy kimono that bared her sensational legs, sampling her croissant and French press coffee while scanning the *Journal* headlines. Her critical focus would be on the work week ahead, not on what had or hadn't happened the night before. Yes, his breadwinner wife liked to set high standards, but it was only from herself and her office subordinates that she demanded something close to perfection—not, thank God, from her doting househusband.

There was, in short, an excellent chance that Chris would once again skate free, as he had so many times before. It was just like Wally, his old college roommate, had said after getting his first glimpse of Kelly on her Facebook page: "You've fallen into the fucking honeypot, you lucky bastard!"

It was true then, and it was still true now.

CHAPTER TWO ~ DANCING BACKWARD

Actually, it was thanks to Wally that Chris had met Kelly in the first place. It had been toward the end of senior year, and, tired of hearing him complain about not having a girlfriend, his roommate had recommended an off-campus ballroom dance class. "It's a perfect deal for bashful guys like you," Wally had explained. "This old lady instructor keeps rotating partners, so girls just keep walking into your arms, one after another. You got some uglies, some cuties, and some real hotties, too, I shit you not. All you have to do, my friend, is show up."

There had been only one certifiable hottie in the crowded community center that night. But even that elite category didn't begin to describe the visual impact Kelly had made. At a distance, she was impressive; close-up she was lethal. She reminded Chris of Tinker Bell all grown up, with her pixie-cut, white-blonde hair and a tight-cinched lime sweater dress that emphasized reckless curves above and below. By the time he was finally paired off with this ravishing angel, Chris' heart was at full gallop—among other symptoms produced by her sudden proximity. As a fairly tall guy, he was startled to find that, in her high heels, she looked him straight in the eye—and to devastating effect, her own eyes being gray with glints of gold, star-lashed and brimming with mischief.

"I hope you're not going to faint on me," she said, playfully sizing him up after his gulped hello. This was a girl who obviously enjoyed her devastating effect on males.

"I'm—I'm sorry. It's just that—"

"It's perfectly all right." She made a throaty chuckle. "You don't have to talk. Just hang on tight when the music starts, and you'll get through this, I promise you."

On the instructor's shouted cadence, all the couples moved into a fox-trot. Chris managed to keep his eyeline safely above the breathtaking scoop of her neckline, but his mind had totally blanked on the basic step that had just been demonstrated, so he let himself be guided by this goddess. It seemed to work, though he felt like an oversized marionette in her capable hands. If she let go of him, he thought, he might just collapse in a heap.

"Very good," she told him when the music stopped. "You sure you're a beginner?"

"Totally. But you're sure not. I mean, it's pretty obvious. So, I mean, uh, why are you—?"

"Why am I taking this class? Because I love to dance, always have. Ballet as a little girl, before I started growing these and they made me switch to gymnastics and cheerleading. But lately it's been mostly ballroom. The problem is—boo hoo!—I haven't got a steady partner. So you might say I'm here on a hunting expedition, or you could even call it stalking. Speaking of fair game, I especially like them shy—dance partners, I mean—and at least my height or taller." His voluptuous pixie poked him in the chest with a lacquered fingernail. "You are unattached?"

"Me?"

"Yes, you."

"Absolutely."

"Absolutely? Is that beyond totally?" Another husky chuckle sent shivers down Chris' spine. "You know, you're awfully cute when you blush. I'm Kelly, by the way." She stuck out her hand, the fingers exquisitely tapered, he noticed, and the nails French-tipped.

Chris took the lovely hand carefully, almost reverently, stifling an impulse to kiss her fingers. He did manage his own one-syllable name without stammering. Then they were dancing again and he was back in perfumed heaven with her breasts compressing their pliant heaviness against his chest as she purred into his ear, "Just yield to me, sweetie, and I'll guide you."

Alas, after only a few more minutes of total bliss, the next rotation was called and Chris found himself pulled into the desperate clutches of a heavyset girl who moved like a truck.

But that was okay. Because, just before they were separated, Kelly had leaned close and breathed into his ear, "Don't forget me."

As if!

When the class ended, Chris stood on tiptoe, anxiously scanning the rapidly dispersing couples, but Kelly was nowhere to be seen! How could that be after what she'd said? But, incredibly, with a tick of the clock, his Tinker Bell had turned into Cinderella and vanished from the ball, not even leaving a glass slipper behind. Should he rush outside, check the parking lot and sidewalks or—

"Psst! I'm right behind you."

Chris whirled about, his features betraying a split-second transition from despair to euphoric relief. "Thank God!" he said without thinking.

"You didn't think I'd run off and leave you?"

"Well, yes, I was sort of worried there for a second." Chris shrugged, trying to downplay his obvious panic just now. Could it be, based on maybe five minutes together, that this creature already exercised such a frightening sway over his emotions? Yes, he thought, that was exactly what had been demonstrated just now, and they both knew it. And Kelly's impish grin conveyed that she was quite pleased with the results.

She took his arm now and spoke sweetly: "Let's go for coffee. I want to talk to you."

*

Ravished by a patrician.

Chris had come across the phrase in a Victorian novel and never forgotten it. Those four words encapsulated a favorite fantasy, one with many variations. For instance, a Hungarian countess might whisk him right off a Parisian sidewalk into the back of her dark Rolls Royce saloon, and he'd never be seen again. Or he might vanish to the world after being hired to paint the portrait of a reclusive baroness in her Bavarian castle.

Could something fantastic like that happen in real life? Of course not. But Kelly's invitation to have coffee had summoned the old fatuous daydream out of its crypt, and her first words to him, as they settled at a small table at the nearest Starbucks, further inflamed his hopes:

"Want to know why I picked you, Chris?"

"Picked me, uh, to have coffee with?"

"Don't be obtuse. I wasn't joking back in class when I told you I was hunting for a possible steady dance partner. I was quite serious. I'm not saying you're the one, please understand that. But you are the only guy out of that whole class who got invited to coffee by yours truly and who's sitting here beside me practically wagging his tail. Now, Chris, would you like to know why I picked you? Or maybe you'd like to take a guess?"

"Because... um... I'm such a stud?"

The lame joke elicited another of her husky laughs—an overly hearty laugh, Chris thought, obviously intended to deflate his male ego, which it did. How effortlessly this blonde goddess could put him in his place!

"No, that's definitely not the right answer. And that's not the quality I'm looking for either. Guess again."

"Well, you said you like shy guys. And I certainly qualify there, right?"

"Yes, you certainly do, sweetie. And, yes, that's important to me. But that class was full of shy guys. And some of them were cute, too. In fact, there was one absolute hunk actually afraid to look me in the eye. But, no, I have something else in mind besides shyness."

"It can't be because I'm such a good dancer."

"No, it can't. But you're actually getting warm, Chris. Give up?"

"Yes, please tell me."

"It's because you followed my lead."

Chris thought about that. "I—I guess I did. But isn't it the man who's supposed to lead in ballroom dancing? Isn't that what the instructor kept saying?"

"Correct. Only you didn't even try, Chris. From the beginning you let *me* lead." He nodded, recalling his utter reliance on Kelly, step after step. "You always waited for me to draw you into the next step, then yielded to whatever I wanted us to do. There was even one time that, instead of stepping backwards, like the teacher was showing all the ladies to do, I deliberately stepped forward, invading your space, just to see how you would react. And you instantly gave ground, stepping back on your right foot, the correct lady's part." She paused. "You weren't aware of this?"

"Not really. I was just kind of caught up in the moment and your—your—"

"In my female power?"

Chris grinned sheepishly. "Well, yes, that's pretty much how it felt. You told me to hang on and you'd get me through it, so that's what I did."

"And you did very well, Christopher, extremely well for your first time." Kelly's hand dropped, palm down, over his, pinning it flat to the tabletop. Chris stared at this, trying to calm himself. His heart was racing again. Out of the corner of his eye he was aware of her studying him, but she was so close now that he was afraid to turn and look at her.

She went on, more softly and slowly, emphasizing each word: "Here's why I brought you here, Chris, so listen very carefully. I'm looking for a guy who will follow my lead—not only on the dance floor, but in all things. How do you feel about that?"

"How do I feel?"

"Yes. Haven't you been paying attention, Christopher?"

"Yes, I have. It's just that—I'm sorry. It's just that I get all sorts of feelings when I think about what... well, about what you just said."

"Good! Tell me some of them, please."

"Well, I'm excited, of course, and... uh, kind of scared."

"That's honest, at least! I'm glad that I excite you, and it's okay to be scared and to admit it. Because this is a very serious question you're being asked, Chris, and your answer just might affect the whole rest of your life. I'm glad you didn't answer quickly, or flippantly, because if you had, frankly, I would have eliminated you from the selection process. I would have known you weren't a serious person. So, let me ask my question a different way, more of a hypothetical and maybe a bit less scary. Do you think you could possibly be the guy I'm looking for? Someone who could enjoy following my lead in all things, exactly the way you did tonight in dance class?"

Chris' heart rate was spiking again, and a crazy voice in his head had grabbed a megaphone and was screaming into it—*Say yes, you fucking moron!* And truly, how else could he answer her question? He'd never get an opportunity like this again, and he'd never forgive himself if he blew it. But his "yes," when it finally came out, was barely audible.

"You'll have to do better than that, Chris. Look at me, please." He'd been fixated on his pinioned hand again, so he turned and was instantly transfixed by her shimmering gray gaze. "Say it again, and this time don't mumble."

"Yes."

"Yes what?"

"Yes, I think I could be the—the guy you're looking for."

"You could be? But do you want to be, Chris? Would you like to be that guy, my guy, the one who follows my lead—in everything?" She twitched a smile, then lifted her hand from his and dropped it into her lap. "Hypothetically speaking, of course."

"Yes. Yes, Kelly, I would." And then thought, O, my God! Because her unseen hand had moved from her lap to his, and her fingertips were now caressing his already rampant erection.

"Hmm, you are excited, aren't you? Can you get even more excited for me?"

His brain was suddenly freewheeling, unable to form words; and, unable to sustain her point-blank stare, he glanced down at the tabletop, visualizing the electrifying violation that was proceeding just below. Because Kelly had hold of him entirely now, her fingers like an arcade claw machine, squeezing his penis and ball sac through his pants! And, yes, he was definitely getting harder for her.

This is what it feels like to be ravished, he thought in an ecstatic panic, just like in his fantasies, only better, way the hell better, and scarier, too. Because, like she said, this was for real—or could be, if he played his cards just right. But what would she do next?

She provided the answer, suddenly releasing her intimate grip with the throatiest chuckle yet. "I can see I've already scrambled your poor little male brain, Chris. So, let's forget about any hypothetical future, shall we, and just focus on your being my short-term dance partner. I know you're terribly excited, but this is important. Are you able to listen to what I'm saying?"

"Yes, yes, I think so, Kelly. I'll try." Chris felt faint, and his pulse was off the charts, thinking about what had just happened and what hadn't—if she'd squeezed him one more time, he'd have cum in his pants! But he couldn't think about that. He had to purge his mind, calm down, try to concentrate—because she was speaking again:

"That's a good boy. Now, here's the situation. I've got a term paper due for my women's studies class in five weeks, and so far I've only got a title. It's pretty good, though. 'Following Her Lead: Reversing Gender Roles in Ballroom Dance.' What do you think?"

"I like it."

"You'd better! Now when I say Fred Astaire and Ginger Rogers, do you know who I'm talking about?"

"Sure. I love those old movies."

"Well, another positive checkmark for Christopher. And do you know the old joke about how Ginger had to do everything Fred did, only backwards and in high heels?"

"No, but that's very funny."

"It's funny, Chris, because it's true. It's like with everything women do. We have to work twice as hard as men to make half as much, or maybe three-quarters, if we're real lucky. Plus we have to make it all look easy, like Ginger did, while always being ladylike quote unquote and deferential to all the male egos on our way up. But that's not me, Chris. Men better get the hell out of my way—or get stepped on hard. On the dance floor and on the job."

Kelly's eyes had narrowed during this short, impassioned speech, with her mouth tightened and chin thrust forward. Now her face softened again, and her sensual smile returned. "End of sermon—do I hear an 'Amen'?"

"Amen."

"Thank you. Now, again, pay close attention, because this is where you might be able to help me. I've got to finish my report, and for that I need to gather some data. I want to conduct my own role-reversal experiment in ballroom dancing, and for that I'm going to need a partner, one I can train quickly—and, for the right guy, there just might be a special reward at the end of the process." She focused on him, knowing that he was now her helpless captive. "Do I have a volunteer from the crowd?"

"Yes, ma'am," Chris grinned, "you sure do. But if we dance that way in class, won't the teacher object?"

"From now on, I'm your teacher, Chris. We're done with the class, it's served its purpose. Now, on your feet."

"Here? You're not going to start now, here at Starbucks?"

"Are you embarrassed? Or afraid of what those two losers over in the corner will think of you when they see me pushing you around backwards? Yes, right over there, the ones who've been ogling me ever since we walked in."

"I'm sorry, Kelly, it's just that I'm not used to doing stuff like that in public—"

"Then get used to it if you want to be with me. You should be proud to be my guy—or even my girl, on the dance floor—because, believe me, every guy in this place, would give anything to be in your shoes. And by the way, whenever I tell you to do something, Chris—like 'on your feet'—you don't ask questions, you just do it, understand?"

So, right there in Starbucks—with people looking up from their tablets and iPhones to watch—Chris once again became a male mannequin in Kelly's hands. He was carefully manipulated into the correct lady's ballroom position—back straight, chin high, his left forearm and hand draped along Kelly's right shoulder, his right arm extended and his palm wrapped up in her left. Then, as she slowly counted cadence, he was danced backward and guided around in a small circle, with pauses for needed corrections and adjustments before resuming.

After a few arduous minutes Kelly called a halt. "That's it for tonight, sweetie—I just wanted to give you a taste. You're still lurching around a bit, and occasionally I catch you trying to initiate instead of just surrendering to my will. But you'll get better with practice, so don't worry, because you'll be getting lots of practice."

She wasn't exaggerating. The next night, and every night thereafter, Kelly put him through a strenuous hour of what she called "role-reversal rehearsal" in a small practice room in the basement of the college music department. She'd kept things pretty basic, with only two dances—foxtrot and rhumba—and the same four or five steps in each in various combinations. Afterward, he faithfully practiced those same backwards patterns solo—in his own room, with the door closed to keep Wally from making wisecracks.

Chris had never worked harder or concentrated more on anything in his life. He lived for each crumb of encouragement Kelly tossed his way during rehearsals—like "Doesn't that feel better, Chris, when you step gracefully under my arm then turn back with that sweet expression on your face?"

Three weeks later she pronounced him ready, and they made their debut at an after-hours club in a downtown loft. Kelly had prepared Chris that the other couples would all be women—"Yes, it's one of those kinds of clubs." She even bought him a suit for the occasion, but Chris figured nobody would be looking at him, not with Kelly in her sensational side-slit sarong and four-inch platform heels.

Suddenly, then, at a signal from the girl deejay, who already had their music, Chris was being pulled onto the floor by his glamorous partner. Initial polite applause from the all-female onlookers exploded into raucous cheers when they assumed their opening reverse-gender ballroom position. There was more cheering during the foxtrot as Kelly steered Chris backwards around the small square of polished parquet, especially each time she spun him this way or that. But the women really got off on their final dance—a rhumba to the slow, sensuous beat of "Besame Mucho." There were shouts of "You go, girl!" as Kelly, head high, back arched and hips undulating, glided smoothly through a series of Latin combinations, sending Chris to and fro like a yo-yo. By the time the song was almost over, the crowd had closed around them, clapping in rhythm. Finally, as Kelly bent her compliant partner backwards over her outthrust knee, they simply went wild.

In the giddy aftermath, Kelly had rushed him out the door and into her nearby car. She turned to him then, clearly delighted at how well it had gone. "We did it, Christopher! Do you know that song from *My Fair Lady?* God, I feel just like Henry Higgins after the ball!" Taking his face in her palms, she kissed him passionately, filling his yielding mouth with her warm breath and thrusting tongue. Chris had nearly passed out—not so much from his own excitement as being utterly engulfed by hers. And there was great relief, too, after all those intense weeks of practice and secret spasms of shame and humiliation over allowing Kelly to usurp his manhood. In this shared moment of triumph, all those fears and doubts receded, as if they'd never been. Kelly had never looked more dazzlingly beautiful or powerful, and Chris had never been prouder of anything in his life.

Kelly had driven him straight back to her apartment—a place he'd never been allowed to see. In the fevered language of his fantasies, Chris had thought of it as "The Lair of the She-Creature." And there she'd delivered his promised reward, taking him to her bed for a night of prolonged abandon and almost unbearable intimacy. Never had the lovesick young man experienced so many orgasmic moments, ecstasies both major and minor, so many that he lost track of the number and forgot even that they'd been all hers. That fact seemed almost irrelevant, as again and again he was swept up in the raptures of his earthly goddess. What greater gift could a man be given? At some point, certainly, Chris knew what he wanted from the rest of his life, and that was to belong to her body and soul.

CHAPTER THREE ~ NEXT STEPS

Only a week after that unforgettable night, Kelly took the first of several major steps that would ultimately make Chris' dreams come true—at least a reasonable facsimile of those dreams. Doing housework had never featured in his fantasies, that's for damned sure, but Kelly made it clear this would be an intrinsic part of his support role in her life—if he was to move in with her for the final two months of senior year.

Chris accepted—of course he did!—and was pleasantly surprised to find Kelly far less demanding in her home than she'd been on the dance floor or in the rehearsal room. So long as Chris kept her apartment reasonably clean and uncluttered, took good care of her clothes and served breakfast and dinner on time and to her specifications, Kelly seldom complained. Her laser focus during those two months was entirely on academics; and when she had her face in a textbook or her laptop, Chris hesitated even to ask a question.

Kelly's hard work paid off. She graduated *magna cum laude*, with a double major in business administration and accounting. She explained to Chris that, absent any tangible career prospects for himself—he'd fallen more than a few credits short of graduating—his clear future path lay in following along to wherever her future took her—then devoting all his efforts, just as he had these last two months, into helping her succeed.

In other words, he'd be following her lead once again. Kelly simply assumed his acquiescence on the matter, and rightly so. From their very first dance, Chris realized, she'd been in complete control of his movements.

Then she sat him down in front of her laptop to show him the top four job offers she'd been considering. All were attractive, entry-level management positions, all required relocation, but the one from a prominent hotel and resort chain carried the most impressive title—associate director of sales and marketing in their West Coast office. Salary and benefits were generous enough, she explained to Chris, so she could afford to keep him at home full-time.

Another strong inducement for Kelly was the extensive travel involved, some of it to the international resorts she'd be selling as holiday and convention sites. Chris wondered what he was supposed to do all those weeks she'd be away, but he only nodded as she clicked a few keys to bring up an acceptance email she'd drafted earlier. "Let's go for it, sweetie!" she said, then hit "SEND." She didn't often ask his opinion on things.

Six weeks later, as she'd promised her new employers, Kelly hit the ground running, while Christopher began unpacking the dozens of boxes and trying to put things where she'd most likely want them, and making sure to hand her a glass of wine when she got back each night with her dinner at the ready.

It was incredible, when you stopped to think about it, all that had happened in such a short time—and almost exactly according to the plan Kelly had outlined over coffee after that first dance class. She'd gone hunting for a guy to follow her lead, dragged him back to her lair, remade him to suit her needs, and six months later almost to the day she'd installed him in a new high-rise condo in a new city while she began climbing the corporate ladder.

Kelly's three- and six-month performance evaluations were spectacular, and if all continued to go well, she confided to Chris, she intended to make an honest man of him. At the end of her first year she got her expected promotion to West Coast sales and marketing director—by far the youngest ever to hold that title, and the first woman; and they married the following spring in her parents' church in suburban Minneapolis. "Now you truly belong to me," the bride said as she kissed him at the ceremony. It was Christopher's own thought, and the abiding wish of his heart, even though he knew it was not a two-way pledge. Never once had Kelly said, or implied, that she belonged to him.

The tough part came after the wedding and the Caribbean cruise honeymoon as Chris settled into the role of full-time househusband. Once he'd gotten through his very manageable daily schedule of housework, he had no idea what to do with himself. He missed his wife something fierce, but she didn't want him calling or texting unless it was really important. Which left him often wandering empty rooms like a zombie, waiting for his goddess to bring him back to life.

The only public part Chris was called on to play in Kelly's career climb was to show up with the other corporate spouses at high-level shindigs and holiday parties, smiling and nodding and being generally presentable. Mostly, Kelly had him stand at her side and keep her wineglass filled.

"I know you get bored, sweetie," Kelly told him once, "but you're a big part of the success I'm achieving here. Of course, I could do it without you, but, believe me, it would be a lot harder."

But Kelly did not wish to seem uncompassionate. So, knowing her husband was only a few credits short of earning his graphic arts degree, Kelly gave him permission to cut back on his daily chore list so he could take the necessary online courses. And later, when he complained of feeling housebound, she added that he could get a part-time job, preferably in his field, so long as he was back home in time to clean up and fix dinner.

Chris was grateful for these generous concessions and promised Kelly to act on them. They showed him that she still cared deeply about his happiness and felt bad that he had to spend so many hours on his own, without the guiding presence of his goddess. But, as her executive career continued its steady climb, leaving Chris with even more time on his hands, an odd thing happened. He began gradually to adjust and soon found himself enjoying his stress-free, laid-back life as Kelly's househusband—or, as he put it to his old friend Wally over the phone one day, "her kept man." Once he'd run through his morning chore list—now further reduced thanks to Kelly's generosity—he basically had the rest of the day to himself. Truth was, once he'd gotten Kelly off to work, he often went back to their king-sized bed and watched TV or played games on his iPhone.

All in all, what was not to like about his new life? He'd been ravished not simply by a patrician, but by a blonde goddess whose sexual magnetism surpassed even his wildest teenage fantasies. He figured, of course, that when she was away, all kinds of well-heeled and opportunistic guys were hitting on her and probably offering her lavish presents, but he trained himself not to think about that. After all, he was the one she came home to. And even if their marriage these days was seldom as exciting as on that first incredible night she'd seduced him, and even if his career-obsessed wife no longer had time to take him dancing, backward or otherwise, Chris still considered himself, to paraphrase Wally, the luckiest bastard on the planet.

These pleasant recollections gave Chris a sense of contentment bordering on complacency as he drove Kelly home through the early morning gray from the airport. Soon enough, up ahead, here came the freeway sign for their offramp. Chris took another mirrored glance at the back seat and was reassured to find that his goddess was still sleeping.

*

But Kelly was not asleep back there. She'd been awake the whole time, and, like Chris, thinking back along the three-year timeline of their relationship and seeing much the same landscape and landmarks, but reaching very different conclusions. One of these was that Chris was only partly to blame for the recent decline in the performance of his duties as househusband, and in his overall level of service to her.

She had let it happen through conscious neglect. Males, she knew, require almost constant female supervision if they are to function at their best. She'd started off right with him, taking charge right from the beginning. Teaching him to dance backward, and then to do it in public, had been a wonderful object lesson in yielding to her will, as were the strict rules she'd applied when she'd moved him in with her, the way she'd talked down to him whenever necessary, even inserting the word "obey" into his wedding vows while deleting it from hers.

But as she had begun to focus her time and energies almost entirely on her career, Kelly had relaxed her controls over him—and, worse, actually eased his daily regimen. And Christopher had taken advantage of it, as any male would, getting by with the least amount of submissive service. In fact, he might well have gotten away with it for some time to come.

But his timing had been badly off tonight, and in more ways than one. During the last ten days and nights she'd had dealings with several extremely charming and powerful men, and one in particular who was still texting her. Aside from that, Chris' inexcusable failure to pick her up on time had led directly to her witnessing the dark-haired domme giving the boot to her cute male slave. And that, in turn, had not only excited Kelly by displaying the naked exercise of female power, thereby awakening her own natural dominance, but reminded her of the effectiveness of strict female rule on masculine behavior.

How, she had wondered, would raven-haired Cougar Domme handle a recalcitrant male like Christopher? Kelly had some definite ideas about that, and she intended to implement more than a few of them—and very soon.

And, perversely, she thought, Chris would be the happier for it. A stronger hand on a tighter leash, stricter supervision over his daily life, these things would not only improve the discharge of his domestic duties, but make him happier and more fulfilled as her submissive. And, Kelly firmly believed, absolute submission to her will was the destiny he secretly craved. In any case, it was the destiny he was going to get.

CHAPTER FOUR ~ WARNING BELLS

Kelly's first impression on entering her upscale condo, after directing Chris to take her bags into the bedroom, was to be suitably impressed. The hand-knotted Persian carpets in the entryway and living room had been vacuumed, the oak flooring along the perimeters reflected the faint early-morning light through freshly Windexed windows, all the tabletops were dusted and clutter-free. Hmm, had she misjudged her boy?

Farther on she noted the bright bouquet of spring flowers on the dining room table, and a few steps toward the open kitchen revealed spotless granite countertops and a shiny stainless-steel sink free of dirty dishes. And was that a trace of lavender vanilla she detected in the air?

"Like it?" he said, suddenly close behind her. "You know how much I want to please you, Kell—"

"Very nice, Christopher." Kelly stepped around him, seeming not to notice his arms opening for the welcome-home hug she'd denied him at the airport. "I'll just have a quick look around while you unpack my bags. Don't forget the carry-on. I've separated the clean things to be put away or ironed from the dirty ones, but you'll have to sort out my lingerie and delicates for hand-washing."

"You want me to unpack for you?" Chris said stupidly.

"I don't know why I didn't' think of it before, since I'm always on the go. It will be a good thing for you to learn, Chris, as it will save me so much time." This was absolutely true, Kelly thought, stepping into the kitchen for a closer look. The task of packing and unpacking

21

for her business travel should have been Christopher's from the beginning.

"Okay, okay," he said, heading for the bedroom.

Feeling a bit underappreciated, are we? Kelly thought as she stooped to look beneath the overhang of the lower kitchen cabinets. Just you wait. You ain't heard nothing yet.

After checking along the baseboard, Kelly straightened to inspect the double sink, then, in quick succession, she checked the under-sink utility cabinet, oven, refrigerator and freezer. She found exactly what she expected to find—abundant confirmation of the trace evidence she'd been seeing and overlooking these many months. All the puzzle pieces were fitting together, and she could see clearly now what needed to be done. There was no need to postpone his reckoning.

*

In the master bedroom, as he carefully unpacked his wife's big rolling bag, Chris was growing more and more nervous. He'd been sure Kelly would be so exhausted from her long, twice-delayed flight that she'd head straight for bed. Instead he could hear her high heels clicking through the adjacent rooms, stopping then moving on. Cupboard doors were being opened and shut, one after another. She'd never done anything like this before—an honest-to-God inspection!

As the sounds continued, apprehension grew into a sinking feeling in the pit of his stomach. His panicky, last-minute cleanup couldn't stand this kind of scrutiny, not in a million years! And now she'd moved to the little service porch and was opening the big storage closet. Still she said nothing. Chris, waiting for the axe to fall, couldn't stand it anymore.

"Can I help you find something?" he asked, appearing behind her again.

"No, not really. I just thought you might have done more ironing."

"Well, there's, uh… your Calvin Klein pantsuit back from the cleaners, and I, uh, I picked out that celadon blouse as an alternate for tomorrow along with your gray tweed pencil skirt. You've worn that combination before, so I laid it out on the bed for your approval. And you'll find several more skirts and blouses freshly ironed and hanging in the bedroom closet."

She gestured at the big wicker ironing basket, which was actually overflowing. "What about all those?"

"Uh, any in particular, Kell? I could get started right now, if you know which ones."

"I wanted them all done and hung up in my wardrobe, Christopher. That way I could click through them and choose."

"Right. I'll make that top priority."

"No, don't worry about it now, I have some other priorities to discuss with you. Have you finished my unpacking?"

"Um, well, I wasn't sure about some items, whether they need to be dry-cleaned or just pressed and hung up."

"Another topic for later. I'll give you a quick tutorial on packing and unpacking for me, and you can take notes. Right now I want you to pour me a glass of wine. Do we still have any of that Malbec? Yes? Good. Fetch it, then come sit beside me. We need to have a little talk."

*

Along with a sense of foreboding, Chris felt something akin to relief as he carried the two glasses of Argentine red wine into the living room where Kelly had kicked off her pumps and settled herself in one of the armchair recliners in front of the big screen TV, hiking up her skirt and tucking her legs beneath her. Relief, because this moment of truth had to come, he knew, like the welcome thunderstorm that clears the air after an oppressively humid afternoon. Once Chris had been skewered by a few well-aimed lightning bolts from his goddess, things could go back to normal.

He handed her the wineglass, then moved toward the matching armchair.

"Did I tell you to pour yourself a glass, Chris?" This was said in an offhand way, yet immediately set off little warning bells in Christopher's brain. "You must listen more carefully. Now go pour it back in the bottle and come right back to me." Kelly flexed her top leg outward, pointing her nyloned toe across the room at a tiny oval footstool covered in floral needlepoint, a family heirloom wedding present from one of her aunts. "You can slide that over and sit here in front of me where I can see you better. I don't want you in the armchair just now."

"Sure, okay, I just thought—"

"You've been doing far too much thinking on your own, without

23

getting input from me, and it's getting you into trouble."

"You know how sorry I am about tonight, Kell. I swear it will never happen again."

"I know it won't. Because we're going to take steps to assure it won't. Now do as you're told, and next time I tell you to do something, don't acknowledge it with a 'Sure, okay.'"

"Sorry, Kell."

Chris hurried into the kitchen, energized and oddly excited by her words, even more by the imperious tone in which she'd said them. How long since Kelly had talked down to him like this? Long enough that Chris had nearly forgotten what it felt like, and how much he used to crave it—that feeling of delicious surrender to her will. But it all came back now in a rush as he fumbled through the kitchen catch-all drawer for the tin funnel, then snatched it out and used it to empty his glass back into the bottle.

A few seconds later he was seated on the absurd, child-sized footstool, staring upward at his exalted goddess. Of course she'd arranged the seating to maximize the power differential between them, rendering her husband a lowly commoner before an enthroned queen—a queen, the top buttons of whose blouse had become unfastened, revealing the deep cleavage. But it was more than stagecraft, Chris knew; Kelly really was a superior creature, he truly believed that, and it did feel right to kneel before such beauty and magnificence. She had always had that effect on him, from the first moment till now.

Chris had a flashback to another time when he had performed a ritual obeisance before Kelly and maybe two hundred witnesses. It had happened at their wedding reception at her parents' country club. A gilt chair was placed on the dance floor, Chris had escorted Kelly out to the chair, she gliding in her fabulously expensive strapless ivory silk gown. After hitching up the mermaid dress a bit to seat herself, she pointed for him to kneel then lifted the flared hem, exposing a lace garter. Chris' task was to slide the garter reverentially down her smoothly muscled thigh and calf until she could step out of it and fling it to a gathering crowd of unmarried males, including several little boys.

The really exciting part, however, had come afterward. "I think everyone liked seeing you on your knees before me," she'd giggled into his ear, seriously tipsy on Mumm's Cordon Rouge. "I know I did. And you know why, Chrissy Poo? Cuz that's how the entire fucking wedding ceremony should have been conducted—with you at my feet." Kelly had paused for a hiccup, then went on, slurring her words a bit: "Just like when I taught you how to dance, remember? You follow, I lead, always and everywhere. You do 'xactly as I say, while I do 'xactly as I please."

Her playful proclamation ended with a mock-serious suggestion that he commit it all to memory. But there was no playful expression on Kelly's face just now. The look she cast down on him was stern and unrelenting, like a judge at a criminal sentencing. "This talk is long overdue, Christopher, and you know it. When I said you were getting into trouble, it wasn't just about what happened tonight. It goes way back."

"I don't know what you mean," Chris lied. "I… I shop and cook and clean for you, Kell, and—"

Her scornful laugh silenced him. "If that's true, why did I hire a professional cleaning service back in February when I invited half the office over?" She took a sip of Malbec, then added, "and a caterer, to cook and serve?"

"Okay, I admit, I don't exactly do a professional job, but—"

"You've been doing a half-assed job, even for an amateur. A piss-poor job." Kelly paused, noting the disapproval on Christopher's face at her use of crude language, something she seldom did. "But, then, you've hardly been trying. Certainly not after I gave you permission to cut back on your chores, which has to be among the stupidest things I've ever done."

By this time Chris knew the game was up. His only remaining play was to show his contrition and beg her forgiveness. He was already in an ignominious position on this ridiculous footstool; now, if only he could make himself cry somehow, he could bury his face in her lap and appeal to her maternal instincts. But while he was debating his stratagem, Kelly moved first.

Her long dancer's legs unfolded swiftly, scissoring down on each side of his head as Kelly sat forward. That quick, Chris found himself caught in the luscious wedge of her spread thighs, his vision tunneling down through the open folds of her hiked-up skirt and coming to rest on a shimmering triangle of lavender satin trimmed in lace and escaping blonde curls.

"Are you staring at my crotch, young man?" she asked in mock outrage.

"Oh, God!" Chris moaned, not in reply, but in abject surrender to her female power. He felt engulfed by Kelly now, his senses overwhelmed. His memory flashed back to those long, intoxicating smother sessions she used to subject him to in her college apartment, sitting on his face while she studied or chatted idly on the phone, all the while manipulating his rampant cock to the brink of orgasm only to deny him, again and again, for her own amusement.

What was her devilish game this time? For he knew his comeuppance was surely at hand. But was Kelly only going to toy with him, or was she truly angry, like the wrathful goddess Juno in the lithograph over her headboard?

What she did was reach down and cup his chin, then tip his face upward. "Look at me, Christopher, like a good boy, not at my panties. Understand?"

She had used her whispery, bedroom voice, and Chris felt a creeping excitement. "I'm sorry, Kell," he said.

"Now, do I have your full attention? Just nod for 'yes.' Good. I'm going to begin by telling you just a few of the things that caught my eye on my little walk-through just now, okay? Let's start in the kitchen, shall we? The countertop was wiped clean—good job! If you don't count all the crumbs and crud under the toaster and blender. But the baseboard running under the kitchen cupboards—bad job! That's filthy. Of course, you have to get down on your hands and knees to see it, which I guess you don't bother to do. There's a film of grease on the stovetop and on the side of the cupboard right beside it. The inside of the microwave is spattered with what looks like tomato sauce. In fact, all the cupboard doors have little specks and spots on them; perhaps you need to have your eyes checked. What else? Oh, yes, that darling little African violet on the kitchen windowsill—a present from my assistant, Todd, remember?—it's dead or dying. The dishwasher—hmm, what could be wrong with the dishwasher? Nothing, except it's packed with dishes, still warm from drying and ready to be put away. Why would that be, Chris, unless you let them accumulate for days, then did a last-minute washing? The refrigerator shelves all need cleaning, scraping in some instances, especially the vegetable bin. There's something rotten in there, but it's hard to tell what it was. I found several Tupperware containers from before my trip, ancient leftovers. Please throw them out. The freezer needs a thorough cleaning, too. When did you do it last? Don't answer, since you probably don't know. The dish towels are clean—I don't think you even use them—but they're folded sloppily. If you can't do a decent job of folding, iron them so they're presentable."

Kelly sighed and sat back, leaving her legs astraddle. She enjoyed another taste of wine before resuming in the haughty tone of voice that always quickened his pulse:

"As for dusting, well, you've done precious little of that. I didn't check the bookshelves in the bedroom or my office, but I can see a layer of dust on the sideboard from here. Can't you see the dull cast over my crystal ballerinas? Oh, and please, Chris, grab the 409 and a rag and clean around the doorknobs, all of them, in the hallways and the bedrooms. I've been looking at those hand smudges and smears for weeks, but I waited, hoping you'd take care of it while I was gone. Alas, alack—and I didn't even venture into the bathrooms. I could go on and on, but do I really need to? I'm not a neat freak, Chris, you know I'm not, but I swear I'm going to become one until the standard of your housework improves drastically."

"Okay, of course, you're right, Kelly, but—"

"But what? Am I being unfair to you? Perhaps you're thinking, 'Well, after all, she's the one who told me I could slack off in my chores,' right? But that's not what I said, Chris. What I said is you could cut back a bit so you'd have time to take online classes to get your diploma—or look for a job in your field, before your computer graphics skills become outdated."

"I did look at some online classes, Kell, honest, and I wanted to ask you about which ones you thought would be best."

"That must have been ever so time-consuming, poor darling! What about a part-time job? How many interviews have you lined up?"

"None yet. I sent my resume out to some local ad agencies and PR shops, and I'm waiting to hear back."

"Which agencies?"

"Well, uh, there's Dayton Reynolds. They do a lot of local TV spots."

"You mentioned Dayton Reynolds like a month ago, Chris."

"I did?"

"Yes. You said a friend of yours got a job there."

"Right, that's the place."

"So how long has it been since you queried them?"

"Couple weeks, I guess."

"Oh, Christopher, this is simply pathetic!"

Kelly scooted forward again, taking his face in her hands, not in the tender, caressive way she often did before kissing him, but roughly, preventing him from evading her piercing gaze or the questions she began snapping at him:

"How much sports did you watch while I was gone?"

"Not a lot, but some, you know."

"What about the NBA playoffs?"

"I watched some of them."

"Which ones?"

"Boston and Golden State."

"Is that one game or two?"

"Two."

"That's all? You didn't watch any others?"

"Highlights, you know, on 'Sports Center.' And I did watch some complete games, but mostly on the DVR—after I'd done my work."

"Did you invite anyone over to watch with you? You know, some of the guys from your favorite sports bar down the street? Am I going to find bottle rings on the end tables and peanut shells under the sofa cushions?"

"No, Kell! I don't go to O'Malley's anymore, not since you forbad it, and I wouldn't invite anybody over without telling you first."

"Telling me? Don't you mean asking me first?"

"Yes, that's what I meant. But absolutely I wouldn't do that. No one's been up here but me, Kell."

"That's all very interesting, Christopher." Kelly let go his face, but she wasn't done with him, as he well knew. "But now I think it's time to sum up, don't you? While I've been working as hard as I possibly can every day—not only for myself, but for both of us, thinking that we're a team—remember the way we used to be, with me the leader and you the faithful follower? But instead of supporting me in my efforts, and being someone I can count on, you've been goofing off. Planting your cute little butt in the big fancy recliners I bought for us out of my year-end bonus and watching the big screen TV I'm still paying for, and— what else have you been up to? I suppose you've been checking out all your favorite x-rated sites and jerking off—"

"No!"

"Of course you have, Chris, but I'll deal with that later. The point is, you probably spent all of twenty minutes thinking about a job, if that, because why the fuck should you?

"You've got a great gig here, don't you, with your Type A, executive wife as your meal ticket? Life is good, right? Honestly, Chris, I'd think you were smoking weed, the way you've let everything slide. Don't worry, I'm not accusing you of that. I'd have smelled it by now, if you were. But what the hell were you doing with all your time? You did almost no ironing or dusting, none of the weekly maintenance routines I helped you set up after our honeymoon. You bullshit me about being a good boy whenever I called, then thought you could fool me with a last-minute cosmetic cleanup, then a few shots of lavender mist and a five-dollar supermarket bouquet."

Kelly shook her head in disgust, having evidently completed the litany of his failures. Chris didn't dare move, or even breathe, as he waited for whatever was to come. He didn't have to wait long, for, quite deliberately, Kelly raised her right hand and, from her superior position, slapped his face, harder than she'd ever done before.

When his vision cleared, the first thing Chris saw was Kelly's right hand cocked in midair. He flinched, reflexively throwing up his left forearm.

"Don't you dare try to protect yourself from me!" she screamed down at him. "Anytime I slap you or punish you, Christopher, you are to take it like a man, understand?"

"I'm sorry, Kell!" Chris dropped his arm, clenching his face against what was to come. The second blow was harder than the first, whipping his head rightward and setting the whole left side of his face afire. It took several seconds for Chris to gather his scattered wits and, careful to keep his arms at his sides, focus fearfully up at his wrathful Juno again. The instant he did so, Kelly grabbed a fistful of his shirt front, just the way gangsters did in old movies, and yanked him close, so that her face was only inches from his:

"That shocked you, my little man, didn't it? Good, it was meant to. You've become extremely complacent, Christopher, and lazy, and disrespectful, and I'm afraid it's going to take some very harsh measures on my part to turn you back into the man I thought I married, a man worth keeping. Don't fidget when I'm talking to you!

Don't move your eyes from mine! Don't even blink! You need to listen very carefully to what I'm saying. The long free ride is over, understand me?"

"Yes, Kelly. I'm so sorry."

"Of course you're sorry, you've been caught out, and reprimanded, and soundly slapped, as you deserve to be. And you actually think that saying the magic words 'I'm sorry' will make everything okay again, and Kelly will forgive you, like she always does. But it's going to take a hell of a lot more than empty promises this time."

Kelly let go of his shirt front and pushed him away, then sat back again in the big chair, breathing deeply to compose herself. But it wasn't really fury that she was letting subside. Oh, she'd been angry enough at Chris, and still was, and he'd be experiencing a great deal more of her wrath in the days to come. But the primary emotions that had been rampaging through her these last few minutes were sexual. She'd experienced a dizzying rush of erotic power from slapping her husband with such unrestrained force, not just the act itself, but the realization that she had the authority to do so—anytime she chose. This is how Cougar Domme must have felt dropkicking her slaveboy.

Be careful, came a whispered warning from somewhere within Kelly. You are entering the "dark side" of dominance, allowing cruelty in the mix.

Well, suppose she was? Isn't this what she truly wanted, and what Christopher needed, deep down? Hadn't the thrill in striking him, then rebuking him for daring to protect himself, been precisely because she'd crossed the line into forbidden territory?

The fact was, so long as she'd pursued that domineering course with Chris, they'd prospered as a couple; but the instant she'd relaxed the grip of her leadership, their tight bond had begun to unravel, and Chris had reverted to type—into male sloth, self-indulgence, rudeness, forgetfulness, even lying to her to cover his sins, as he'd dared to do tonight.

No, she wasn't going to miss this irresistible erotic adventure, and she was certainly not going to let Christopher escape the exquisite fate she'd envisioned for him from the very first, a journey into ever deepening submission.

Meanwhile, Chris was continuing to look up at her, full of his usual wonder and adoration, but mixed now with real fear. A good sign, and long overdue!

She drained the glass of wine and, with a deep sigh of satisfaction, set it down. She was ready to resume their "little talk," and was able to do so now in calmer tones.

*

"Do you remember on our wedding night, Chris, when I had you get down on your knees beside the bed and repeat your vows to me, and then all the other things you said to me that night?"

"Of course I do," Chris said, heartened by this new tone of tenderness. Please, God, let the storm be over!

Gently now, she tipped his face to hers so she could look right down into his submissive soul. She'd taken him to the very brink, she sensed, right where she wanted him. "Then repeat your sacred vows to me, Chris. I want to hear you say them again."

Chris felt an upwelling of raw emotion. Her angelic face, only inches away now, was growing blurry. He blinked rapidly, trying to clear his vision, and began haltingly:

"I... I pledge to love... and honor... and worship... and... and..."

"Yes, say the next word, sweet boy. Look into the eyes of your goddess and say it!"

"Obey! I vowed to obey you!"

"Very good! And for how long did you vow to obey me, my darling?"

"For as long as I live, Goddess Kelly! I vowed to obey you forever!"

With this final remembered promise, Christopher's face finally crumpled and his desperate tears burst forth. He looked away then, wanting to hide his wretchedness from her, yet reaching blindly for her in his great need and crying out her name. Kelly guided his questing hands around her hips, then twined her fingers in his curls and tugged his head forward, docking it snugly between her thighs.

She had planned to reduce Chris to exactly this abject state, and was gratified at how easily she'd brought it off. And yet she couldn't help noting how pathetic he looked as he shuddered and sobbed beneath her. Christopher was, after all, a tall and good-looking man, intelligent and accomplished in many things. Kelly wasn't the only woman who coveted him on sight, she knew. And yet he'd let himself be turned into little more than a lady's servant—and wasn't even doing a passable job at that!

How could she not lose all respect for such a broken man, even if she'd done the breaking? Especially when she matched him against one or two alpha male executives she'd met on this sales trip, men whose easygoing machismo had made her go all-girlish. Luckily for Chris, Kelly relished the power rush she got from reducing him to this groveling status—snorting and snuffling between her legs like a rooting pig, and blubbering like an inconsolable child. And so, despite her contempt and the almost irresistible urge to degrade him even further, Kelly murmured comforting endearments as she caressed his curly head.

"Let it all out, little boy," she heard herself cooing. "Don't hold anything back from your goddess."

"Oh, God, Kelly, I'm so sorry!" Pleading his case between sobs, Chris rolled his face to look directly up into her eyes. "Can you ever forgive me?"

"Well, we'll see about that," she said noncommittally.

Kelly did not doubt that Christopher's remorse just now was genuine, unlike the counterfeit versions he'd tried on her earlier. But what was to come next? His need for her just now was acute—for her punishment, a small sample of which she'd already given him in lieu of forgiveness, and, of course, for the ultimate sacrament of worshipping her womanhood. She could hear a quickening in his breathing as his face burrowed between her legs; hear him mewling like a babe for mother's milk.

There'd be no stopping him now short of another bell-ringing headslap. And she was out of the mood for that. It had been an exhausting day, and, frankly, Kelly wanted nothing more than to recline farther back, open her legs wide and give herself completely to her desperate boy.

He didn't deserve it, of course. And she deeply wanted to deny him his ultimate reward of oral service tonight. But she couldn't deny herself—not for another fucking minute. She needed to push his cunt-seeking little face into her sopping-wet pussy lips this instant!

She ordered him to beg her for what he wanted. And when he started stammering like a fool, her patience ran out and she screamed at him to peel off her pantyhose and panties and get to work.

CHAPTER FIVE ~ GIRL TALK

His alarm went off at six-thirty, as usual. This was to give him enough time to shower and shave, brew and serve Kelly her wake-up coffee, then fix her breakfast and lay out her clothes. She needed to walk out the door, briefcase in hand and dressed to kill, no later than eight.

But not this morning! Chris thought, as he silenced his cell phone's mindless chiming. Although Kelly hadn't revised his standing orders, there was no way she'd be going into the office at her usual time. When she'd finally succumbed to sleep after her last operatic climax, it had been around five. Then Chris, his testicles swollen and penis still ramrod stiff, had lain awake maybe another forty minutes, wishing like hell he could finish himself off. Which meant he'd gotten less than an hour of sleep!

So, now, instead of rolling out of bed, he merely lolled his head sideways on the pillow to check on Kelly. Maybe he could whisper in her ear, get her mumbled permission to go back to sleep.

Only she wasn't there. Her side was empty, the covers thrown back. He cocked an ear for any sounds emanating from the bathroom, heard nothing. In fact, the whole place felt empty. Chris sat up, groaning at the effort. His balls ached, his cock was still rock hard, his face was sore where he'd been slapped, and his whole body was begging for a few more hours of precious sleep.

He lurched into the master bathroom. Kelly's makeup kit was open, jars and tubes and wadded tissues strewn about, the curling iron at an angle, the cord dangling, not neatly coiled as Chris always kept it. She was up and gone. Without waking him. Why?

He staggered out to the kitchen, found a scribbled note on the counter:

"Early meeting. Do your chores. Talk later."

Curt and crisp. No endearments, not even an acknowledgment of all his efforts on her orgasmic behalf, while being denied, as usual.

On the other hand, there might be some positives to be extracted from her note. An early meeting meant Kelly's laser-like focus would be directed back on her job, not on the many shortcomings of her househusband. Which meant, in turn, that all those little threats and nasty innuendoes last night about dire consequences ahead for him might come to nothing. As had happened before.

If he didn't goof off today. If he didn't go back to bed, as he was dying to do, but got busy with his chores, as per Kelly's scribbled instructions. If he scrubbed and cleaned all day, blue balls be damned!

But first, with a small sigh of relief, he poured himself some French press coffee—she'd made it herself, for the first time in his memory—and sat down in the breakfast nook. Before launching into frenetic activity, he wanted to think back over the events of last night. The severity of some of the things she'd done and said, treating him with ill-concealed disdain at the airport and with open contempt here in the apartment, troubled him deeply. From the very first, at the dance class, Kelly had worn her natural arrogance lightly, spiced with affection and mirth, and Chris had loved that about her. Never before last night had he been made to feel so utterly inferior in her presence.

It had culminated in her greedy use of him for her own pleasure.

Indelible images of rough, early morning sex still swam in his head, and had pervaded his dreams before the alarm went off. It was not unusual, after a week or more away, for Kelly to be especially demanding in bed. But this morning she'd turned tigress, gripping and grinding his face with frightening ferocity.

It had begun with her sprawled back on the big recliner, then migrated to her big bed, one climax segueing into another, with his face clamped firmly in place throughout. Several times he'd gotten slapped for slacking off, or coming up too often to gulp air.

But it had been pretty awesome, Chris had to admit, as he sipped his coffee, being the focus of such a total female frenzy. By the time she was finished with him, Chris had been dizzied with desire.

Which was of no concern to Kelly. He was not permitted even to mention it. For Chris, sexual relief was a seldom thing indeed, entirely at her whim.

No wonder he'd masturbated when she'd been out of town. Three times, in fact, the first after he'd discovered a pair of her soiled panties under the bed and made the mistake of inhaling their potent fragrance.

Had she left them there on purpose, knowing he'd succumb? Whatever, she'd somehow divined his transgression, making the veiled threat of punishment to come. "I'll deal with that later," was how she'd put it.

Chris didn't like the sound of that. Kelly had hinted in the past about fitting him for a chastity device; he'd assumed she was only teasing. But if that was what she seriously had in mind this time, he determined that he was going to absolutely refuse.

He'd danced backward to her tune all this time, but a guy had to draw the line somewhere, and having his cock locked up was definitely one thing Chris was never going to permit.

Just because he was by nature bashful and self-deprecating—two qualities that had apparently attracted Kelly to him—that didn't make him a doormat or a milquetoast.

In fact, it probably only made him normal. Like all those lovesick boys who'd been following her around since preschool, to hear her tell it. And all those businessmen who couldn't say "no" to her convention and resort sales pitches.

In Chris' opinion, Kelly Ann Sheffield could turn most guys, young and old, into fawning lackeys. God knows, he'd seen it happen in restaurants, hotels, on the street. Waiters, cab drivers, doormen, passersby; anywhere she went, heads swiveled, and men lost the power of coherent speech, their brains turned to silly putty.

So, maybe he wasn't, by nature, a true submissive. Maybe he was just an average guy, a bit more laid back than most, who simply lacked the *cojones* to stand up to a blonde bombshell with an empress complex. He'd agreed from the first to follow Kelly's lead, and he'd kept on doing that rather than risk losing her.

Odds were, if she demanded he wear a chastity device, he'd back down on that, too. So, if he wanted to avoid that fate, his best bet was to avoid a showdown, to placate her in every way, starting with housework.

He finished his coffee, wolfed down a day-old muffin he wouldn't have dared serve Kelly, and then got up to begin his work, his fatigue temporarily lifted by his resolve and the new hope that inspired it.

This time when his goddess came back home, he vowed, the entire condo would sparkle, including the baseboards and those silly crystal ballerinas.

*

Kelly had scheduled a morning meeting with her sales team, assuming her flight would arrive on time the night before. But she'd just canceled it en route to her health club. There was a much more important meeting on her mind this morning. Important enough to get her out of bed and out the door after scant sleep.

Since joining the Muscle Factory, the local fitness mecca, three months earlier, Kelly had been back only once, preferring to train at home or in the small basement gym her company maintained. She liked being looked at, but not endlessly ogled when she was working out, and the popular health club seemed to be a combination shark tank and meat market. Everyone was always checking out everyone else, when they weren't admiring themselves in the wall-to-wall mirrors.

But the one time she had dropped in, she'd met a young woman with a body even more spectacular than hers, at least in Kelly's view. Carmen Gallegos was a sultry-looking Cuban from Tampa with flawless skin that shone like molten gold under the gym lights. Her breasts were only papaya-sized, but the rest of her was fully packed and pumped and ripped like a fitness-model cartoon.

Kelly had made Carmen's acquaintance from an adjoining elliptical and learned, after a few polite queries, she'd placed in several physique contests and triathlons and gone on to win a bunch of money on the "Ninja Warrior" TV show.

"I'm not surprised, Carmen," Kelly had said in frank admiration. "Your physique is incredible. And from what I've seen, you're outworking everyone in the gym."

Carmen had acknowledged the compliment with a high-wattage smile. "Thanks, Kelly! You're not too shabby yourself. In fact, what do you say we trade bods, a straight-up swap? God, what I wouldn't give for a pair of gynormous *chi-chis* like those!"

"I'd do that deal anytime, Carmen. I'm tired of being top-heavy."

"You lying bitch! I bet you love every incredible inch! What are you, Kelly, like a double D?"

"Double-G," Kelly said, laughing. "And, yes, they're real."

"*¡Dios mio!* Believe me, if there was a machine in here that could build me a rack like that, I'd be on it, all day, every day. Trouble is, the more pec work I do, the smaller mine get."

"Yours are lovely. And your ass—"

"Don't tell me, I know. It's a thing of beauty—I mean booty."

"Well, it puts mine to shame."

"It should. I work on it every damned day from every fucking angle. I'm hitting everything extra hard right now because next season on the show I'm supposed to be competing against the guys, and I want to whip their asses!"

With this goal in mind, Kelly learned, Carmen was at the club every single morning, unless she had a contest or a TV shoot. And Kelly was praying she'd be there again this morning as she pulled into the gym lot. She desperately needed to talk to another woman about Chris and her new plans for him, and when she ransacked her memory for a likely candidate, Carmen was the first and only name that popped up.

It wasn't just the way the Cuban girl strutted her stuff—though Kelly liked that about her—but the insolent way she treated her male workout partner, a Latino bodybuilder like herself, small of stature and large of muscle.

The guy was actually kind of scary-looking, with an Aztec warrior face, shaved head and gang-style tats up and down his bulging arms. But what stuck in Kelly's memory was the doglike way he'd followed Carmen around. He'd answer her cell phone and take messages when she was exercising. When she finished a set, he was ready with towel and water bottle. Whenever she snapped an order, he jumped to obey—adjusting a weight or digging into her gym bag for a compression sleeve or whatever. On heavy lifts he acted as spotter, shouting encouragement. But he went way beyond that. He wiped down each bench before she used it and readied each new piece of equipment, enabling her to move through her complicated routines with very few delays.

In many ways, Kelly thought, it had been like watching Cougar Domme work out with her Muscleboy, minus the butt-kicking. And, since Cougar Domme wasn't available for a consultation, Carmen

Gallegos seemed an excellent alternative.

If she wasn't out playing Ninja Warrior or flexing for a camera.

But, to her vast relief, Kelly spotted Gallegos almost at once. She was on a treadmill on the far side of the crowded gym floor, her arms and legs pumping and ponytail flying as she outpaced all the other runners. And hovering close by with towel and water bottle was her dutiful Aztec.

Then, as Kelly drew near, she had another piece of luck. An older woman staggered off the treadmill beside Carmen's. Kelly moved toward it, but Carmen's workout partner got there first, quickly accelerating as he upped the speed controls. *Damn!*

"Hector, get the hell off right now! Can't you see that beautiful lady wants to use it!"

It was Carmen to the rescue, bless her! She'd seen the whole thing and now flashed Kelly a smile as Hector leaped off, apologizing profusely as he backed away.

"No, *estúpido!* Set the speed for her first—exactly how she wants it."

"Yes, move it back to a slow jog," Kelly said, adopting Carmen's high-handed tone, and then, when Hector instantly complied, pointedly not thanking him. It was a test of sorts; Kelly was curious to see how the Cuban girl would react to another woman presuming to boss around her boyfriend, if that's what he was.

Carmen's pouty, sensuous face split wide with a big grin. Apparently she approved.

In motion, her body was even more sensational than Kelly remembered, her flagrant curves showcased by a skin-tight, pink sports bra and sweat-soaked yoga pants. She pitched her voice loud enough to be heard over her pounding pace on the conveyer:

"It's Kelly, right? You haven't been around much. What gives?" She paused, then went on: "Hey, you want Hector to wait on you, too? We could give him a big thrill."

"Actually, Carmen, I didn't come here to work out." To emphasize the point, Kelly switched off the treadmill.

Carmen looked instantly wary and slowed her own speed. "What for, then?"

"I came here hoping to talk with you."

"About what?"

"About my boyfriend. I want him to obey me, the way yours

does."

"You think Hector's my boyfriend?"

"Well, I want to ask you about that, too. But I really need your advice."

"What makes you think I could help with your boyfriend?"

"Because of the way you've got yours—whatever he is—trained. He not only does what he's told, he anticipates your needs."

"You mean like this?" Carmen switched off her machine and, coming to a sudden standstill, reached back and closed her hand around a just-uncapped Dasani bottle Hector was extending toward her.

Kelly shook her head in admiration at the perfectly timed demonstration. "That's exactly what I want from my guy! How do you do it?"

Carmen took a swig of water then reached back again, this time for a towel, with which she proceeded to wipe herself down while looking thoughtful. "You think maybe I should write a book?"

"If you do, I swear, I'll buy dozens and give 'em to all my girlfriends. No, what I should do is make them buy it. I mean, it's women who buy all the books, so you'd have a best-seller!"

"The thing is, Kelly, I can't write for shit, but I talk good. Hey, you want a smoothie?"

"I'd love one. I skipped breakfast."

"I've got a half-hour or so before my Pilates class. Why don't we take this outside where it's private?" Carmen hopped off the apparatus and tossed her towel in the air, knowing Hector would catch it. "Pick a flavor as we go by the bar, and Hector will bring them to us out on the deck."

A moment later they were seated outside in umbrella shade, sipping their health drinks. Carmen restricted herself to a low-carb, raspberry smoothie, while Kelly indulged in a peanut buttery protein shake. Hector stood nearby, obviously ready for his next command.

"We're going to make girl talk now, Hec." Carmen pointed to a far, unshaded corner of the terrace. "Go stand over there, and I'll signal you if I need anything. And try and look casual, for chrissake."

Hector turned and, spreading his lats, moved off in a typical bodybuilder strut. Reaching the designated corner, he took up station, slouching a bit and staring over the parapet at the morning traffic.

"Won't he get sunburned?"

"Maybe," Carmen said, spooning out a raspberry. "So what? Ignore him. He's parked."

"Parked?"

"Yeah. Like sometimes I go to a restaurant with my girlfriends, and I have Hec wait outside. He's used to it."

"He waits the whole time?"

"Sure. An hour, two hours, it doesn't matter. He knows he's not to move. Don't you make guys wait for you, Kelly? Isn't that what they're for?"

Kelly chuckled. "Yeah, I used to—a lot! But in sales, I'm afraid it doesn't work."

"Good thing I'm not in sales! In my world, I tell a guy to do something, he better fucking do it now—or else! But sometimes, you know, I get tired of giving orders? So when Hector's done all his chores, I like to park him at home—sit him in a chair or just shove him into a corner, tell him not to move or else, just to get him out of the way so I can forget he's there."

"That doesn't sound like he's your boyfriend, right? So what exactly is he to you?"

"We'll get to that. For now, let's just say he's my male, and I can do whatever I want with him. I learned that early, even before kindygarten, no shit. I'm talking like back in the sandbox here. There was this one boy, he'd do anything I said, so I stuffed his mouth with sand and told him to swallow it. He tried, he really did, before he gagged and threw up in his mouth. And later on, starting like in fourth grade, boys were fighting each other after school to carry my books and following me home like stray dogs. My dad had to chase them off. And this was even before I got my tiny tits and big ass."

By that time Kelly was laughing too hard to comment, so Carmen continued: "Something tells me that you know just what I'm talking about."

"That's part of why I'm laughing. You're not going to believe this, Carmen, but I've got a sandbox story of my own, I really do—one I haven't thought about in years. In third grade we had this exchange student from England, Trevor something or other. And he kept following me around, just like the boys your dad chased off. So one day after school, I was practicing on the monkey bars in the sandbox and Trevor appears and just stands there, staring through his thick glasses at me hanging upside down with my underpants showing. So I pushed him down in the sand and took off his glasses and sat on his face."

"How long?"

"It could have been like fifteen minutes, since the place was deserted, and I got a kick out of it. But I think it was like a religious experience for poor Trevor, because for years after he went back to England he was still writing me these ten-page love letters. I don't know how he got my address, but thank God my parents never read them!"

"Good old face-sitting, isn't it romantic? The thing is, Kelly, if a woman unleashes her full erotic powers, it doesn't matter what age guys are, or how macho they act or how big their biceps are. I mean, look, in six months I turned Hec from Macho Man into basically my bitch, and I'm still not done with him. Okay, now tell me about your naughty boyfriend. What's the deal with him anyway?"

With that irresistible invitation, Kelly launched. It felt so good finally to open up to another naturally dominant woman about all her frustrations with Christopher, both recent and of longstanding, and, most of all, her last-minute qualms about how far down into submission she really wanted to take him, and how fast.

Carmen was a good listener, but she couldn't help breaking in with pithy comments and anecdotes of her own. Kelly couldn't remember when she'd laughed harder, or had more fun swapping stories, than she did with the vibrant sexy Latina—and they weren't even drinking! Halfway through the detailed narrative of the backward dancing, Carmen interrupted again:

"Whoa, Kelly! You're telling me you did all those things to Chris, and he was fine with it, and yet you're still not sure what his primary status is in your life?"

"I guess I do know, but I'm just hesitant about going the rest of the way with him."

"You know what I think?"

"What?"

"You've already got the game, you just need the name. You know, to make it official."

"Maybe you're right."

"Of course, I'm right. And all that stuff you told me about how he's been slacking off on his chores, and sometimes talking back, and even questioning your authority, that's just typical male insubordination—and easy to fix."

"It is?"

"Yeah."

"How?"

Instead of answering, Carmen pointed to Kelly's cell phone. "You got a voice recorder app on that?"

"Sure."

"How long is it good for?"

"Two hours, maybe more. I added extra memory because I use it a lot in meetings."

"Two hours should be enough. Here's the deal. In a couple minutes I'm going to tell you to switch it on, and then I'm going to start talking. This is like my favorite topic, and I can go on all day, and I don't want you to have to take notes."

"What about your Pilates class?"

"Screw Pilates! This is way fucking more important. I'm serious. Look, if I haven't run out of material in an hour, I suggest we take this to lunch. I know a great organic salad place just down the street."

"Okay," Kelly said, experiencing a giddy euphoria at all she was about to learn. She'd have everything professionally transcribed, word for word, and commit it all to memory! After she was armed with all of Carmen's dominant weaponry, and began to use it on Christopher, the poor guy wouldn't know what hit him!

She couldn't wait!

"But first," Carmen said, draining her smoothie, "let's give Hector a break, since you're so worried about him. I'll send him on some errands or maybe home to clean the bathrooms with his SpongeBob toothbrush."

*

It was around two o'clock when they polished off their second pitcher of sangrias, which they'd progressed to after their California monster salads. At this point both women were seriously buzzed and hoping the fresh air and the two-block-long walk back to the health club might sober them a bit. The opposite seemed to happen, however, as they began giggling over the silliest things; and when Kelly tripped slightly over a sidewalk ridge, Carmen caught her, then broke into the chorus from the Sonny and Cher super-oldie, "I Got You Babe." Kelly tried to make it a tipsy duet, but she was a dancer, not a singer, so she linked arms with her new friend and taught her the "Follow the Yellow Brick Road" dance step all the way to the health club parking lot.

Here, after exchanging sincere hugs, they somehow got caught up in an endless loop of ridiculously phony Hollywood air kisses, which cracked them both up even more.

"Enough, Kelly girl, enough!" Carmen said, pulling away and holding up her Fitbit watch. "I really, really gotta go now."

"I know you do, Carmen, but wait! I have to tell you one more teeny, tiny little thing, which I believe I overlooked."

"I think you said everything there is to say and then some, but okay. What is it?"

"You, my friend, are *muy fantástico!* Did I say that right?"

"Not bad for a *gringa.* Now, remember, I want regular reports from you."

"Right, regular reports. Mustn't forget those."

"I don't care if you're right in the middle of a heavy scene with your guy, and you draw a complete blank and wonder what the fuck Carmen would do. Just text me and I'll text you right back and tell you what the fuck I'd do. Remember, Kelly girl, we're all in this together."

"That means so much, Carmen, so fucking much! I'm serious now, even if I still sound like totally wasted. I only wish there was something I could do for you."

"I been thinking about that. Maybe—assuming any of this works with your Christopher, which I know it will—what you could do is try and get me a special discount at one of those fancy resorts you sell."

"Okay!" Kelly said, delighted to be able to reciprocate. "I got you, Babe!"

CHAPTER SIX ~ THE TIPSY TANTRUM

Around two-thirty that afternoon Chris ran out of steam, exhausted from housework and lack of sleep. Yet, as he put down his Swiffer mop and dropped into one of the recliners, he had a feeling of deep satisfaction at how much he'd gotten done in his six-hour whirlwind of dusting and sweeping, cleaning and scrubbing, picking up and putting away.

If he could work just half this hard every day, he thought, he could make their condo a showplace. And think how proud Kelly would be of her househusband.

Of course, that was impossible. Not just the physical drudgery, but the mental tedium of it would cripple any man. Which is why, Chris reminded himself, all his previous resolves to tackle the housework in a systematic way had failed so miserably.

All the same, it felt really good to have pushed nonstop through so much of his chore list, and he couldn't wait for Kelly to come home and see all he'd accomplished.

Reclining all the way back now, he groped on the side table for the remote. "Sports Center" would be on—it was always on—and he could catch up on the NBA scores. But the device was just out of reach. If he sat upright, he could grab it; but he was too tired to make even the slight effort required. Maybe in a few minutes, he told himself...

An hour later he was snatched from a deep, drugged nap by a text message alert. It could be only one person. Chris had lost touch with his college friends, except Wally, who didn't text; and now that he'd stopped going to O'Malley's, his social life was nonexistent. Kelly seemed to like it that way.

He fished the phone out of his cargo shorts and read her message:

I'll be there in five minutes. When I open the door I want to see you at my feet, kneeling on the little rug, naked, head bowed.

PS. Not kidding!

Holy shit! Christopher thought, jerking abruptly forward in the chair. What's gotten into her? If she hadn't added "Not kidding," frankly, Chris might have dismissed it as a prank.

But he knew he dare not. Not after last night. He'd better play along with a straight face till he figured out just how serious a deal this was. He wasn't wearing that much anyway. A faded Mumford and Sons T-shirt and threadbare khaki shorts, going barefoot and commando as usual around the house.

But his casual attitude deserted him the minute he stripped off his shirt and shorts. It did affect his psyche, not just getting naked, but doing so in obedience to her texted command. And, for sure, his purple-helmeted soldier was taking the message seriously, already uncoiling for battle as Chris padded toward the front door and knelt down as specified on the little rag rug just out of the door's inward arc.

Now what?

Bow your head! came the immediate answer from his annoying submissive conscience. *Do exactly what she said!*

So he did, but the pose felt phony. And a lot of other things, starting with awkward and ending with ridiculous. Kelly could be many things, but one thing she always was, Chris had thought, was a class act. Requiring her husband to do such a demeaning thing—prostrating himself by the front door in a bizarre tableau—didn't fit her image at all. Her style of dominance had always seemed elegant and even a bit tongue-in-cheek, distinct from the online netherworld of whips and chains and fetish gear.

But if all that was true, why was his penis fully erect now, and his heart beating like a jungle tomtom?

Calm down, he school himself. One way or another, Kelly was just messing with his mind. Her idea might be to keep him groveling here a lot longer than five minutes, maybe even for an hour or two, afraid to move a muscle.

Then, when she finally showed up, she'd have a hearty chuckle at his expense.

But Chris was wrong about that. Right around five minutes into his estimated countdown there came the distinctive clunk of the elevator's arrival at their floor, followed by the smaller clunk of the door sliding back. Kelly usually preferred the cardio workout of walking or even running up all five flights, but not today, because the steps Chris now heard on approach were definitely hers.

She wasn't in heels, though; she'd changed into flats or trainers, as usual after work.

He grew even more excited, knowing she was right outside. He pressed his forehead against the carpet as the door creaked and swung open, bringing in the hallway draft. He caught her scent, enhancing his arousal; but he remained perfectly still in his abject posture, head down, eyes shut, pulse hammering away.

"Very good, Christopher." Her voice came from directly above him, but there was something slightly off about it, kind of a lazy sound. Then he realized what it was. She'd been drinking.

A shoe slid under his nose. Chris opened his eyes to see the gray, jaguar-printed toe of her Nike trainer.

"Kiss my foot!" she commanded, her words slurred.

Chris obeyed, savoring the pungent odor through the nylon mesh. As his kiss turned passionate, she giggled and withdrew her shoe, replacing it with the other. He resumed kissing till it, too, was withdrawn.

"Good boy. Now look up at me."

He twisted his gaze upward. Kelly towered above him, statuesque in skintight zebra-striped leggings and a neon blue sports bra with custom cups cantilevered outward. Her gorgeous, grinning face was definitely flushed. None of it matched her message about a morning sales meeting.

"This is what I wanna see from now on, Chris, whenever I come home. My houseboy, my househubby, whatever the fuck you are, down there buck naked, ready to slobber on my shoes. And don't think I'm joking, because I'm fucking serious about this. Even if I come back after five minutes, you still get your ass down there, understand?"

"Yes, Kelly," Chris said, realizing now just how far gone she was. Her speech was not merely sloppy, but crude, not at all like the honors grad who could talk rings around everyone they met.

"And it's not only when I return that I want you here on the floor," she was saying now, "but every time I leave, got that?"

"Yes."

"Good. Now turn around."

"What for?"

"Don't question me! Just do it! Show me your ass!"

Chris kneewalked around in a half-circle, not only confused by the way he was being treated, but offended. It was bad enough that she was drunk and slurring her speech, but she had no right to shout at him and be abusive. Then he heard her snicker. She was laughing at him, too!

But Kelly couldn't help herself, as she stared down at her naked househusband with his pointing penis and his exposed ass-crack and his face still blotched from being bitch-slapped last night. How easily he'd let himself be reduced to this groveling, pathetic state. Yet it made her feel so sexy and powerful to see him like this, cowering wormlike beneath her. He was finally finding his proper station in life.

Maybe she should buy those stripper shoes, after all.

On her sales trip, web-surfing one night in her hotel room in the Canadian Rockies, Kelly had come across a pair of eight-inch, silver platform sandals. She'd quelled the wild impulse to order them. But now, as she looked down on Chris, a series of erogenous spasms rippled through her, and she decided to go ahead and get them. Stomping around like a diva atop those glittery, sexy stilts, she'd be nearly half a foot taller than Chris, diminishing him even more.

Carmen had been right, Kelly thought. Males really were unstable, inferior creatures. Six months—that's all it had taken Carmen to turn Hector into her little bitch. Kelly ought to be able to accomplish the same thing with Chris much faster, considering how far down that road she'd already taken him. And, without further ado, she was about to get started.

Slowly, carefully, she drew back her muscular right leg, taking dead aim. Then, with a little hop and a squeal of pure delight, she kicked her naked and kneeling househusband in the ass, just like Cougar Domme had done to her cute, collared slave. And just like him, Chris launched forward to land facedown with arms outflung.

"My God!" Christopher yelped. "I can't believe you did that!"

"Believe it, babe!"

47

"But why, Kelly?" Deep hurt showed in his backward stare, and Kelly didn't doubt that he was in considerable pain. But she suspected the deeper injury was to his dignity and masculine pride, her real targets. "Why would you do that to me?"

"Because I can." Kelly left it at that, omitting the rest of her thought, which was: *Because I can do anything I want with you, anytime I want.* That statement of fact would come later—perhaps tomorrow, certainly in the next few days—after she'd taken Chris deeper into his submission to her.

"But if you really wanna know," she added breezily, "I got the idea at the airport last night—from this cougar bitch with tits almost as big as mine. So you see, sweetie, getting your ass kicked is your own damned fault—for not being on time to pick up your goddess. And don't give me that accusing look or I'll do it again! I swear I will!"

"I'm sorry, Kell."

"You better be! Now follow me!"

Abruptly, Kelly headed for the living room, her unsteadiness adding extra hip-sway to each step. When she glanced back to see if Chris was enjoying her tipsy strut, she was shocked to see him getting to his feet.

"Who the fuck told you to stand up? Get back down there and crawl after me!"

Chris dropped to the floor, then, under her hard-eyed scrutiny, began to crawl slowly toward her, his ass still aflame from her kick. With each degrading lurch forward, a single phrase repeated in his mind:

She can't treat you like this.

But, of course, she could, and he damn well knew it.

Way back at the start of things, he'd told himself that Kelly wouldn't really make him dance backward in public. But, of course, she had; indeed, she had reveled in his public exposure.

He could forgive himself for not asserting his manhood back then. But this might be, literally, his last chance to stand up to her and demand to be treated with at least a modicum of respect.

It's now or never!

But, to his eternal shame, Chris kept crawling toward the glorious, arrogant creature who stood waiting by the easy chair, tapping her foot impatiently.

"You'll have to learn to crawl faster," she snapped. "Now take my hand."

Realizing what she wanted, Chris helped ease her down and backward into the big chair, which opened out into full recline.

"God, I'm so fucking tired," she said, rolling her head side to side on the headrest to ease tension. Then she stopped, focusing across the room at the distressed oak sideboard. "Hey, looks like somebody dusted my ballerinas."

"That would be me," Chris said proudly.

"You actually did some dusting for a change, sweetie?"

"Yes, Kelly." He was encouraged by the softening of her tone, from scathing contempt to mild sarcasm.

"And what about your other chores? What else did you do for Goddess Kelly?"

"I worked hard for you all day. I did a lot of ironing—there's still more to do, but I had to scrub the baseboards and the stove and—"

"Please, spare me the incredible details. Your goddess is not exactly in the mood to hand out gold stars. Whatever you did, that's what you should be doing every fucking day. Or you're not working hard enough for me."

That's so unfair! Chris thought. The one time he actually had the condo ready for her inspection, she wasn't even interested.

"What I really want is a drink—not that kind of drink, don't worry, just some fizzy water. Go to the fridge—crawl there and back, it'll give you more practice—and fetch the Pellegrino."

You're not actually doing this, he tried telling himself as he obeyed the absurd directive. And that's how he truly felt—as if he was being operated by remote control, or jerked around like a puppet, just like he'd felt dancing backward.

Whoever was animating him, Chris didn't dawdle; in fact, he crawled back to her even faster than he'd gone, despite having to drag the bottle along the floor. If she expected him to crawl and carry from now on, he thought wryly, she'd need to fit him with a collar like a St. Bernard's and hang stuff around his neck.

He unscrewed the cap before leaning forward on his knees to hand her the cold bottle. She accepted it without acknowledgment, gulping greedily before handing it back. "God, that tasted good. You know what I want now?"

"No, Kell."

"I want you to take off my shoes and kiss my feet. You know

what I like, so take your time and do it properly."

Doing it properly, as Chris well knew, also meant a long and loving foot massage and having her toes sucked as well as kissed. Not that he objected. Ministering to Kelly's lovely feet each night had become a favorite ritual, a time for complete immersion in worshipful service to this incredible female.

And so it was again. Even without her Shea Butter lotion, which he was simply too tired to fetch, Chris became instantly absorbed— and aroused—as his fingers and tongue moved over the perfect contours of her feet. Usually he lost all track of time, so that he couldn't have said if he'd licked and sucked her darling toes for five minutes or twenty-five. But now, after only a few minutes, his hands began moving slower and he caught himself nodding off from fatigue.

He shook himself awake, hoping Kelly hadn't noticed the lapse. He needn't have worried. "That's enough, sweetie," came her next slurred command a moment later. "I'm drifting off. Help me to bed."

Chris had to stand to get enough leverage to bring her up into sitting position, but she was too far gone to care, or even notice. What she did notice, as she came unsteadily to her feet, stretching and yawning hugely, was Christopher's penis, at full rigid salute despite his exhaustion.

"Well, well, well," she said, seeming to perk up a bit. "What have we here?"

Her fingers encircled his engorged shaft and, almost absentmindedly, started stroking. She yawned again, as if unaware of the galvanic effect she was having on him, especially as she upped the pace. Kelly delighted in teasing him like this and watching him fuck empty air.

And soon enough, despite Chris' best efforts not to respond like a sex-puppet, she had his hips and buttocks flexing and thrusting. A moment later, as she tightened her frictive grip, she heard his breathing quicken into a series of gasps and grunts.

Then she released him; but not as she usually did, at the last possible instant to thwart ejaculation, but well short of that. Chris looked up, startled, to see her stumble sideways and grab the chair arm to keep from falling.

"My God, Christopher, look at me! Too tired even for a bit of edge play. Take me to bed this instant."

She let go the chair arm and sagged against him. Chris caught her and held her up, then began guiding her carefully toward their bedroom. There was no crawling now. He felt a surge of manly pride at the sudden turn of events, despite his penis flopping around in futile frenzy. She still needed him—that's what really mattered, not her occasional temper tantrums.

"Get me closer," she said once inside the master suite. He steered her toward the bed, expecting her to collapse facedown. Instead she made a grab for the nearest bedpost and held on, remaining upright, but only just.

She spoke without turning around: "Undo me."

Chris moved quickly to unfasten the custom sports bra's hook-and-loop closure. From behind, Chris could only imagine those magnificent mounds tumbling free of the supersized cups.

"Now my pants—and panties, too. And no smoochies!"

Chris dropped to his knees and began tugging downward gently on both waistbands at once. But progress slowed over the amphorical swell of her butt cheeks.

"Hurry, dammit!"

He tugged harder, exposing her rear cleavage and savoring the soft sibilance as the cotton-spandex fabric slid faster down her glorious flesh—but, evidently, not fast enough.

"Oh, for God's sakes! Just get out of the way!"

Letting go the bedpost, Kelly toppled sideways, bouncing off the mattress. "Now," she said, rolling onto her back and elevating her legs, "yank them off and be quick!"

Pivoting on his knees, Chris grabbed hold of the bunched leggings and panties and pulled so hard that he toppled backward with them in his grip.

Kelly broke out laughing at his comic pratfall. Chris would have joined in, but he was now transfixed by the vision of his goddess in all her naked splendor. She was lounging back on her nest of pillows with her thighs open to his avid gaze, revealing the holy of holies beneath the luxuriant blonde bush. And higher up, her opulent breasts, gloriously unhammocked and side-sloping, quivered with her laughter.

Chris, still on his knees, was overcome with reverence to be in the presence of such wondrous beauty. How could he have hesitated, even for an instant, to throw himself at her feet and to obey her every command?

He dared to hope that, before she slept, she would permit him again to worship her orally, as he'd done all last night. And, indeed, she was beckoning him forward with her forefinger. In eager obedience, he crawled onto the bed, his head dropping into the glide path between her thighs as he pushed forward toward her nested sex.

"No, not down there." He looked up in surprise to see Kelly's finger summoning him onward, then her arms opening to embrace him. She spoke again, in her sleepy, husky voice, "Come on, come to Mama."

The meaning was inescapable—and mind-blowing! After enduring all those insults and injuries, including face-slaps and butt-kicks, now he was going to get to fuck her! Chris couldn't remember the last time he'd been permitted to enter her fully as a man, or how well he'd performed, but it didn't matter. He was ready now—oh, God, was he ever ready! His exhaustion melted away, and he felt supercharged with energy, like a racing engine revving up at the starting line.

With his pulse pounding in his head, he crawled carefully atop his goddess. She smiled and welcomed him like he was already a conquering hero, her arms encircling his nakedness and pulling him down, her massive breasts cushioning on contact.

Don't get too excited or you'll squirt and spurt before you even get inside!

Chris dismissed the insidious voice of self-doubt. He was not afraid of failing. This was one dance where, by God, he would lead and Kelly would follow. All these years she'd been testing him, waiting for him to throw off his timidity and show himself her worthy champion—the man to whom she could at last surrender! Now, finally, it was going to happen!

Her fingers closed around his swollen shaft as if to guide him into her, as she'd done each time they'd had penetrative sex. But apparently she had something else in mind. To Chris' dismay, using his penis as a convenient handle, she yanked him sideways, then rolled him completely off her. Chris ended up on his back alongside, stunned and confused.

He looked up at her, half afraid to see a living likeness of the wrathful Juno that hung above the headboard. Instead, his goddess smiled down with a sweetness that was positively maternal.

"I'm too tired for that, sweetie. Maybe another time. I want you to nurse me to sleep. We haven't done that in a while, but I'm sure you remember how. Can you do that for me, sweetie?"

Without waiting for his reply, Kelly adjusted him, cradling his head and shoulders in the crook of her strong left arm, then guided his face toward her plentiful left breast. Chris barely had time to open his mouth before he was pushed deep into the pillowing flesh. The last thing he saw before being enveloped was a swollen pink nipple set jewel-like in its aureole of dusty rose.

"That's it, sweet baby," Kelly cooed above him. "Right there. Stay right there, all night long."

But Christopher was already beyond hearing. He felt himself helplessly drifting into an altered state, a state of infantile bliss.

CHAPTER SEVEN ~ RADICAL CHANGES

Chris had gone to sleep in Kelly's arms countless times, and occasionally while suckling at her breast. They both loved this; though usually, after a nice long while, she would push him away or he would gently detach himself.

Not so this night. Eventually Chris had thrashed about, trying to alter position and squirm free. But each time her maternal embrace had tightened and his face had been forcibly guided back to her nipple. At some point he had stopped trying to escape, and, surrendering to his voluptuous fate, had experienced hours of deep, almost uterine slumber.

In the early light, his eyes had opened to see Kelly gazing down at him—like a Madonna in a painting. Overcome with submissive yearning, Chris had curled even closer against her, his fingers and mouth groping anew for her breast. Moments later he began emitting throaty mewling sounds.

Exactly like a feeding baby, Kelly thought. A baby with a hard-on.

She glanced over at the bedside clock. It was quarter past six; they'd been in bed, both of them obviously exhausted, nearly twelve hours!

Sorry, snookums, time to get up.

Kelly had two items in mind for the morning. One was a pre-lunch meeting with her sales staff; the other, which would obviously have to come first, was another no-nonsense talk with her househusband. In both cases she would outline her goals and expectations and make specific assignments.

She separated Chris from her nipple and sat him up. Or tried to, as he immediately sagged against her. He was not merely woozy from too much sleep, she thought, but infantilized from too many hours on her tit. Her surmise was quickly confirmed as she watched his glassy stare slide down from her face to her exposed bosom—and stay there.

She reached out and lightly slapped his face.

"Sit straight and look at me, not at my boobs."

She watched him try and fail, unable to shift his focus from the twin talismans that had him hypnotized. Irritated, Kelly grabbed the top sheet and wrapped it like a sarong around her thrusting torso, the way she'd seen movie actresses do in bedroom scenes.

"Now maybe you can pay proper attention."

"I'm sorry, Kell. All I can think of is you."

"Me and my twins, I know. I was curious about the addictive effects of regressing you into virtual babyhood, but maybe I overdid it. I'm afraid you've suffered brain damage."

"It's not that. It's just—oh, God, Kelly, I love you so much! And I'm so sorry for the way I acted yesterday when you came home, arguing with you—"

"Well, you should be. But all that's going to change. Starting right now."

Chris was startled by the new glint in Kelly's eyes and the sudden schoolmistress tone. Where was the look of maternal radiance that had bathed him just a moment ago, and the soft, soothing voice?

The change was deliberate; Kelly had simply flipped a switch. Last night in bed she'd been improvising, indulging a little fantasy of her own. Now it was time to get back to Carmen's script. She leaned back against the headboard, folding her arms and regarding Chris as though from a great height.

It was a look, Christopher thought, eerily like the imperious stare in the lithograph directly above her. Goddess Juno meet Goddess Kelly.

"As you may have noticed, I played hooky from the office yesterday. I needed a break. But I am going in this morning, maybe a bit later than usual, after I go over some important matters with you."

"I thought we already had that talk, and I promised—"

"Be quiet, Chris! You're not setting the agenda, I am. Things are going to change radically around here—perhaps you've gathered that—and I won't be asking for your opinion, just your compliance. Got that?"

"Sure, okay, Kell, if you say so."

"I do say so. Now, the French bakery, it opens at six, right?" Chris nodded. "Good. So while I shower, put coffee in the French press and put the kettle on, then run out and get a dozen croissants. Do you have enough household cash?" Again he nodded. "If you really hurry, maybe you can get back before the kettle starts whistling. If you can't, don't worry, I'll get it—and paddle your buns later. Now get going."

"Okay, Kell."

"No, not 'okay.' I already scolded you about this yesterday. When I tell you to do something, I don't want to hear any more 'okays' or 'all rights' or 'sures.' They sound lame, like a verbal shrug. It's almost as insulting as 'whatever!'"

"I'm sorry, Kelly. I didn't mean it that way."

"Whatever!" She laughed. "Now get going—and put on some clothes. I don't want to see 'Naked Guy at the Patisserie' going viral on Instagram. Oh, and one more thing. While you're out, I want you to think about the next radical change in our relationship, and see if you can guess what it's going to be. Okay?"

Chris nearly said 'okay' back, but caught himself at the last instant: "Yes, Kelly."

"Then off you go." She gave his bare butt a swat, just hard enough to make him yelp.

*

Kelly was wrong about one thing, Chris thought a minute later, wearing the clothes he'd discarded yesterday as he hurried down the sidewalk toward the corner bakery. Despite what she'd termed his "lame" responses to her direct orders, Chris was always energized when he was doing her bidding. And this morning was no exception.

Even though his errand was only to get back with the pastries in time to snatch the kettle off the flame before it shrilled, he felt like a Knight Errant sent forth to slay dragons for his Lady Fair.

By contrast, those he passed, plodding off to their meaningless jobs or wherever, all seemed gray-faced and aimless, not vibrantly alive as he was at this moment. Chris especially pitied the men. Could any of their lives be half as exciting as his, impelled by the whims of a living goddess?

Still, the surge of euphoric energy couldn't quite mask the incipient panic germinating in his stomach, planted there by her very last command—to think about what kind of radical changes awaited him on his return.

Yet, if he was truly honest, deep down in his submissive soul he'd known this was coming. The insults, the face slaps, even the ass-kicking of the past two days, as hurtful as they'd been, could not erase all the cumulative guilt he felt for a year or more of half-hearted performance as Kelly's househusband. Nor could one day's fanatical housecleaning make up for all the months of neglect of his chores and her property. Despite the seeming unfairness of her harsh remarks, there was an underlying justice to them.

And yet, as he hurried out of the bakery with a big pink cardboard box, his dread of the reckoning to come made him run back to her all the faster. He arrived in time to whisk the kettle off the flame before it could sing, and when Kelly emerged several minutes later, in all her customary loveliness, everything was in readiness. The coffee was ready to plunge and pour into her big breakfast mug, two fresh-baked croissants adorned her plate along with a ramekin of her favorite orange marmalade, and her home-delivered *Wall Street Journal* lay open beside her knife and spoon.

"I trust you approve my choice?" Kelly swept her hands down her hourglass figure to indicate the celadon silk blouse and gray pencil skirt that Chris had previously proposed as an outfit.

"You look sensational, Kelly. I mean, you always do, but those cool gray-green colors—and with your gray eyes and silver-blonde hair—it makes you look kind of like a, uh—"

"An ice queen?"

"I was going to say a Norse goddess."

Kelly nodded, obviously pleased at the compliment as she slipped into the breakfast nook. "You could be right. I mean, I do have all that Scandinavian blood from my mother's side. Not to mention the sort of figure they used to carve on the prow of those old wooden ships."

"I can see it now," Chris said, filling her coffee mug. "Be still my beating heart!"

"I bet that's not the only body part of yours that's beating hard." Kelly grinned up at him over the rim of her coffee mug before turning her attention to the *Journal*. "By the way, you can put the other croissant back in the box. I'm taking them all to the office."

"Okay, I mean, yes, Kelly." Chris concealed his disappointment; he'd been counting on a croissant for his own breakfast after she left. A moment later, having replaced the resealed pastry box on the table, he stood back, awaiting her next instruction.

"Well," she said, regarding him as she licked pastry flakes from her lips, "have you been thinking about what I told you?"

"Yes, Kelly."

"What did you come up with?"

"I—I'm sorry. I didn't come up with anything, I mean like a new rule. But I completely understand why you're, you know, getting tough with me. Remember, I cried about it the other night in your lap, telling you how sorry I am that my performance hasn't measured up to what you deserve? I know I've got to do better, Kell, and I will."

"Blah-blah-blah. That's not what I asked you, Christopher. I asked if you could guess the next rule I have in mind for you, and, frankly, I'm surprised you can't. It should be obvious. In fact, it's implicit in the rule I gave you yesterday." She tapped her head several times by way of encouragement. "Think harder."

Chris tried, but again drew a complete blank.

"Well, maybe you are suffering brain damage from last night. So here's a hint. First, repeat back the new rule you were given yesterday. Can you at least do that?"

"Of course, Kelly. I'm to be on my knees by the door when you come home, and when you leave."

"And how are you to show proper respect when you kneel before me?"

"By kissing your feet."

"And what are you supposed to be wearing when you do this?"

"Nothing."

"Exactly. Now think. I can walk out the door on the spur of the moment or come home without any notice. What are the implications for you?"

"Well, I guess I have to be prepared to react instantly, Kelly."

"Well, I guess you do. But how will you do that?"

"By listening for your footsteps when you're out. Or, if you're here, asking what your plans are."

"But suppose I'm home and get a call and turn to you and say, 'Something's just come up at the office, and I have to leave this instant.' Am I supposed to wait around while you get undressed before you can accompany me to the door and then kneel down to kiss my feet?"

"No, you shouldn't have to wait."

"And I certainly wouldn't. The same applies if I come home without notice. I can't always be bothered texting a warning, as I did yesterday, to give you time to strip and assume the position. You can see that, can't you?"

"Yes, Kelly."

"So what's the solution?"

"I—I guess I should wear a minimum of clothing."

"No, little boy. The rule is simpler than that. You are to be completely naked whenever you are here, by yourself or with me, unless I instruct you otherwise."

"All the time? You don't really mean that, do you, Kelly?"

"Oh, but I do. And the rule goes into effect right now. Take off those ratty clothes this instant and toss them into the trash." She pointed at the tall kitchen wastebasket and snapped her fingers.

Chris hurried to comply, while his head spun with the staggering implications of this latest rule. He'd never dreamed she'd go this far. Seconds later, after depositing his favorite t-shirt and cargo shorts atop yesterday's coffee grounds, he turned to face her, oddly shy about his nakedness in a way he'd never been before.

"Good boy," she said. "How do you like your new uniform? Never mind, I see someone is already answering for you."

Chris glanced down at his penis, which, as usual, was eagerly betraying his submissive excitement at being naked and vulnerable before her. And yet, his dismay was real, too, as he tried now to convey: "But, Kelly, what happens if I'm alone and somebody rings the doorbell?"

"Use the peephole. Send them away or tell them to come back later, when the lady of the house is at home. You're not authorized to transact business anyway."

"What if it's an emergency?"

"Oh, for God's sakes, Christopher. Don't ask stupid questions. I'm not going to throw out all your clothes, just most of them. And you can always tie on an apron," she paused for a giggle, "as long as you don't turn around. Maybe I'll buy you one of those hot pink 'She's the Boss' aprons with a lace trim."

Chris stood there, feeling his stature as a man diminish even as his cock increased the angle of its salute. Kelly might find it all amusing, but an essential part of his personal dignity was being stripped away, and he couldn't remain silent.

"Can I—can I say something more?"

"Of course, you can, though I appreciate your asking permission. I'm probably going to require that in future. What is it?"

"This is more than just another rule you're adding, Kelly. This changes everything between us."

"Of course it does! That's the idea."

"But, I mean, we kind of talked about stuff like this way back in college, remember, when you first moved me into your apartment and we were going over your house rules?"

"We weren't 'going over' anything. I was laying down the law!"

"Okay, I said it wrong, I'm sorry. But you talked about how I had to follow your leadership in everything, but you also reassured me that you weren't into—oh, you know—whips and cuffs and dog collars and kinky stuff like that."

"I know what I said, Christopher. And I certainly didn't rule out keeping you naked, because, if you recall, I did that a lot, especially when I sat on your face so I could play with you. Which, I also recall, you often begged me to do. Isn't that true?"

"Yes," Chris admitted. Just thinking about it now made his cock stiffen even more.

"So what's so different about keeping you naked all the time?"

"I don't know, Kelly, it just is. You're not just taking off my clothes for a while, you're taking them away forever. It's like—like—you don't want me to be a man anymore, but some kind of animal."

"That's actually quite perceptive of you," Kelly said, motioning Chris closer, so she could take his erect penis in hand. "But 'animal' is too vague and nondescript a term, don't you think? Let's just say you're being turned into an obedient little housepet. By the way, I also recall saying that you were not to question my authority to make new house rules at any time."

"I'm not questioning your authority, Kelly. I—I do want to belong to you and to obey you. I'm just wondering if—if—"

"If what?" She tightened her genital grip.

"If—if you're not going too fast on this."

"You want to go back to the way things were, is that it? With you watching TV all day, hanging out with the boys at the sports bar, jerking off to my Victoria's Secret catalogue or whatever the fuck you've been doing?"

"No, no!"

"Good, because those days are over, believe me. If you were my employee, and I was giving you a performance evaluation, frankly, you'd be let go. Is that what you want?"

"No, Kelly! God, no!"

"I didn't think so. But something has to be done—to save our marriage. Harsher measures are called for. Surely you can see that?"

"Yes, Kelly, I can."

She let go his cock and tapped her coffee mug, which was almost empty. Chris blurted an apology and moved swiftly around the table to the French press, which was within easy reach of Kelly. When he'd refilled her mug, he returned to her side.

"Here's the thing. You think we're going too fast, and we haven't even gotten to those harsher measures yet. So far, we're just talking about baby steps."

Kelly took several sips before continuing: "You're a sweet boy, Christopher, and I love you dearly, but let's face it—you have a weak nature and a sneaky side that wants to take advantage of all the privileges and perquisites I've granted you.

"So either we pull the plug, as I said, and I let you go, or we start all over again, with much closer daily supervision and stricter new rules and penalties for the slightest disobedience. Those are the only two choices. Now come closer."

As Chris stepped forward, once again his cock rose obediently into her encircling fingers. "We just spent a very special night together, and one of the reasons for that was that I wanted you to see how completely you can belong to me. That's what you've always wanted, isn't it, sweetie?"

"Yes, Kelly, you know it is."

"Well, now you're going to have an opportunity to belong to me in a whole new way, more completely than you ever have before. Isn't that exciting?"

"Yes. Kelly."

"And we know how your little friend feels about it." Her thumb rubbed the tip of his cock, which was beginning to ooze precum.

Chris felt his entire self, not just his spring-loaded penis, in her controlling grip. And when she spoke next, in a low, husky tone, it was like she was even inside his head:

"I love this feeling of total control, Chris. Don't you love it, too, being so helpless?"

"Yes, oh, God, yes." Chris looked into the smoky haze of her gray eyes and was plunged back into the infantile bliss state in which he'd spent the night. The idea that he could oppose her in any way seemed suddenly ludicrous.

"Now I'm going to give you two more rules, rules that will help you keep this feeling all day, every day. Are you ready?"

"Yes."

"Don't just say 'yes.' Say 'yes, Goddess.'"

"Yes, Goddess."

"Good. That's your next new rule. You are to address me as 'Goddess' from now on, to show proper deference for my superior status. You may also call me 'Goddess Kelly,' but never just 'Kelly,' and certainly not 'Kell.' It's simply not appropriate for you to go on addressing me as though you were my equal. You see that, don't you?"

"Yes, Kell—I mean, yes, Goddess!"

"Very good. As a male, your position in life is to serve the superior female sex, and, specifically, you are to serve me in all ways. Do you understand?"

"Yes, Goddess."

"Do you like saying that?"

"Yes, Goddess."

"You should. Every time you say it, you will be reminded of your proper role in our marriage, which is to worship and obey me. Now, are you ready to hear the next new rule?"

"Can I ask just one more question, Goddess Kelly?"

"Go ahead!" Kelly snapped, annoyed at this further interruption.

"What if—what if, say, we're in a restaurant, Goddess?"

"Of course, if we're out in public, I won't have you call me 'Goddess.' In a social situation, with my colleagues or friends who are unaware of your submission to me, you may call me 'Kelly.' But I expect you to say it with great respect, even reverence. Can you do that?"

"Yes, Goddess."

"Now you're actually getting tedious. You don't need to use my title in every fucking sentence. Here's a simple rule. Whenever you would previously have said 'Kelly,' you will now say 'Goddess' or one of the variants. Otherwise leave it out."

"Yes, Goddess. I mean yes, I understand."

"Good. I'm afraid we've got time for just one more rule. I think this makes number four—you'd better be keeping track. We've covered how you are to address me, but not what I should call you." Chris shivered in apprehension as her grip slid from his penis down to clasp his ball sac. "Any suggestions?"

"Your husband?"

"Sorry, try again."

"Your househusband, I meant."

"Way too cumbersome. Besides, you're not a very good househusband, I think that's been established. And, frankly, I don't think you ever will be. Oh, I may refer to you as my little househubby at cocktail parties and such, but basically I'm stripping that title away from you. Try again."

"Your submissive?"

"Well, you haven't been very consistent there either, though you will be. But let's get back to the fact that you belong to me. That's what makes you go all squishy inside, isn't it." She'd begun massaging his balls.

"Yes, Goddess," Chris gasped.

"So what's the word for someone who is owned by another? Who is someone else's property?"

Chris hesitated.

"You know the word I'm looking for, don't you, Chris? It's been unspoken between us from the very beginning, but you've always known it. Say it now."

"Slave," he said quietly.

"Speak up, you're mumbling."

"Your slave, Goddess. I'm your slave."

"So you say, though you haven't earned that title yet. But I do like hearing it, and I bet, down deep, you like saying it. Tell me again that you want to be my slave."

"I want to be your slave, Goddess Kelly."

"Oh, really? How sweet! Well, I'll definitely keep your application on file," she joked. "But let's put your sincerity to the test, shall we?" She began to squeeze his testicles harder.

"Please!" he begged.

"But I like squeezing them, and, after all, they're my property, so I can do anything I want with them, and with you. Isn't that right?"

"Yes, Goddess. But it's really hurting!"

"And it's about to hurt much worse, because I'm going to squeeze even harder now just to see if you really and truly want to belong to me. If you really want to be my slave, you'll suffer this for me. And afterward, you will say 'Thank you, Goddess.' Are you ready?"

"No," Chris said, sucking air and biting his lip as her grip tightened inexorably. "Please don't, Goddess!"

His plea was in vain. Kelly's fingers suddenly clamped down so hard that he cried out, and then crushed him harder still, till he grunted and dropped to the floor, doubled up in pain. And yet, despite the white-hot ache in his groin, he heard his voice gasp out, an octave higher than normal, "Thank you... Goddess!"

Along with the searing pain came an aftershock of incredulity. How could she have done this to him, been so cruel only moments after telling him she loved him "dearly"? This went way beyond the face-slaps and the ass-kicking.

"There," came her voice, regal and haughty and a million miles above him, "that's what it feels like to be my slave, to be owned by me. How do you like it? Do you want to crawl out the door and run away and never come back?"

"No," he blurted out without daring to think. "No, Goddess."

"Do you still want to be my slave?"

"Yes, Goddess!" *God forgive me, I do! Even after this!*

"Then back on your feet. We're not quite done."

Chris staggered coming up, gripping the edge of the table and actually afraid to meet her gaze. She noted, with some satisfaction, that his proud cock now drooped in defeat. She reached out and seized hold of his genitals again.

Chris flinched and sucked air, remembering the blinding pain of a moment ago.

Kelly nearly told him to relax, that he was quite safe for the moment, but stopped herself. She decided that she liked the way he was quivering with apprehension. "Always give them reasons to fear you," Carmen had advised her.

"I can read your little mind, did you know that, Slaveboy?"

"Yes, Goddess, I know you can."

"And here's what I think you're telling yourself, maybe just whispering, hoping I can't hear your secret little thoughts. You're telling yourself this is all just a fantasy, a kinky, pretend game I'm playing with you, right? Because, of course, slavery isn't legal. Everybody knows that. Not here in our modern world and under our current liberal laws. So you can't really and truly be my slave, can you? Isn't that what you're secretly thinking?"

"Yes, Goddess," Chris confessed, "I have thought that."

"But there's just one problem with that logic. You wouldn't be living under the laws of this city, or this state, or even the good old U.S. of A. Oh, my, no! You'd be living under *my* laws and *my* rule—a naked male slave totally dependent on his owner and totally at her mercy, if she has any. And if I decide to take away your access to TV... and the Internet... and even your cell phone, well! You'd be cut off from the outside world, wouldn't you?" Kelly chuckled as her grip tightened again. "Kind of scary to contemplate, isn't it, Christopher?"

His 'yes' was barely audible. It was more than scary. It was apparent to him that, despite her playful tone, Kelly was actually serious about the kind of enslavement she'd just described—and fully capable of enforcing it.

"Technically, you'd be free to leave—unless, of course, I chain you up." She smiled sweetly as she released her genital grip. "But, in reality, I'm afraid you wouldn't have the will power to oppose me in any way. I believe you're already hopelessly addicted to my power, but if you're not, you soon will be. I'm afraid you will be a broken man, sweetie. That's what makes this all so exciting and so seductive! Are you ready to be reduced to that? Are you ready to be really and truly owned by me?"

Chris had never seen Kelly's face so intensely alive, as if from some inner power surge. Her gray eyes seemed to burn through him like twin lasers. He turned aside, pretending to think, but actually trying to shield himself from her irresistible gaze.

You're in real danger! whispered a warning voice. And Chris knew it was true.

"It's okay if you can't answer right now, sweetie. After all, this is the most important decision you'll ever make, and I want you to think about it all day long. Meanwhile, we're going to put everything on hold here. I won't be back before five, but it could be much later. That gives you a minimum of ten hours to reconcile yourself to your fate. If you decide you're ready to become my full-time slave, I expect you to be naked and kneeling on the floor at five o'clock, and to remain there without moving till I return. Is that clear?"

"Yes, Goddess."

"Good. And when I walk in the door, you don't have to say a word. If I see you naked and in position, I'll have my answer. However, in the extremely unlikely event you decide to decline this once-in-a-lifetime offer, then I'll expect you to have packed up all your belongings—you can use those flat cardboard boxes in the utility closet. Once you're packed, just wait for me, fully dressed, sitting here at the table—not on the recliner watching television. When I get home, we'll talk briefly, and maybe have a little kiss and cry, and then I can make financial arrangements for you according to the prenup I had you sign. Got all that?"

"Yes, Goddess, but—"

"No, Christopher, be silent. I've given you the alternatives, and we won't discuss it further." She stood abruptly, lifting the bakery box by its string loop. As she swept past him toward the door, she reached to give his scrotum a final squeeze.

Chris turned and hurried to catch up, but she held out a palm: "No, stay! You may not kneel and kiss my feet! You have to earn that privilege by being my slave."

Chris felt a sharp pang of regret at being denied what only yesterday he'd considered a degrading ritual. Now he could only stand and watch her go. The instant the door had closed, he missed her terribly.

CHAPTER EIGHT ~ DECISION DAY ~ ONE

On the whole, Kelly was quite pleased with herself as she drove to work. Even the slight flutter of anxiety in her stomach—could Christopher actually be right, was she taking things too fast with him?—only added to her erotic anticipation of what she would find when she returned home.

And, yes, she had thrown a lot at him for one morning—taking away his right to wear clothes, requiring him to address her only as goddess and to bow down before her and kiss her feet every time she went out or came back.

And she'd gone farther yet, risking losing him forever with her departing ultimatum—to accept life as her abject slave or pack his duds and get out. The possibility of losing her darling boy did give her serious pause. What if he wasn't cowering bare-assed by the door when she returned home, what if he was sitting across the room fully dressed with his stuff packed up? Or worse— infinitely worse—what if she really had pushed him too far and his male ego had reared up out of nowhere and he'd simply left, with or without a note?

She couldn't bear to lose her Christopher! She'd been smitten with him at first sight, and those first feelings had evolved over the course of their courtship and marriage into this irresistible desire to possess him body and soul. If that was love, then, yes, she loved him fiercely. And yet, the calculated, high-wire risk of losing him only ratcheted up her excitement.

In fact, just thinking about her coming conquest of Chris was triggering spasms of excitement between her thighs—so much so that, when the freeway traffic slowed to a momentary stop, she couldn't resist slipping her hand under her skirt to caress her wetness. How on earth was she supposed to concentrate this morning on quarterly sales figures and evaluate each of her employees' performance against the goals she'd set for them?

Before she could think clearly about work, she obviously needed to stop worrying over Christopher. Of course he'd be there at her feet when she opened the door. He was already her slave in everything but name; isn't that what Carmen had said? He just didn't know it yet or hadn't fully accepted it. But there was no way Chris could walk out on her, any more than an infant could think of leaving its mother. His dependence on her was total. Hadn't she had to pry his lips off her nipple this morning after the all-night tit smothering?

That had been her idea, not Carmen's, but Kelly very much wanted to tell her mentor about it, and to ask about some other things, and maybe get a bit of reassurance, too. She spoke aloud:

"Call Carmen Gallegos."

The hands-free dial tone sounded, and, after two rings, Carmen's voice came through the car speakers loud and clear:

"Kelly girl, cómo va?"

"Good. Great, actually."

"Did you take away his clothes?"

"I did."

"Did you make him carry them out to the dumpster?"

"Not yet. I gave him a simple choice when I left—this was about fifteen minutes ago. Walk away as a free man or stay on as my slave. In which case—and we both know which case that will be—I'll make him throw them all out. Maybe I'll give him one of my kimonos to wear when he does it."

"What about the other stuff we talked about? What kind of pushback did you get?"

"It was just like you said. He came up with these annoying little objections to every new rule—'what about this, and what about that?'—but it was almost like he felt he had to put up some kind of token resistance. I mean, he sounded so feeble, so adorably pathetic. And his last objection was almost apologetic. 'Do you think, Goddess Kelly, like, you know, just maybe, you might be going a wee bit too fast?'"

Carmen's snort of derision was amplified through the speakers:

68

"Let me tell you something, Kelly girl, you can go as fast as you want with your Chris. Figure out your ultimate destination, how deep down you really want to take him, say, in the next six months or even a year. And then just tell him, Okay, listen up, this is how it's gonna be *starting now*! And you just start enforcing it, in all the ways we talked about. He obeys or else!"

"You're probably right!"

"Of course, I'm right. Unless maybe that would be taking too much of the fun out of it. If you throw him down all the steps at once, you'd miss the thrill of kicking him down each step, one by one."

"Exactly. It's an incredible turn-on. I mean, I've experienced some of this with him before, and with some other guys, especially at the beginning. But, I have to tell you, Carmen, I got an incredible rush out of—shit, this is embarrassing."

"You whipped his ass! Congratulations!"

"No, not yet. But I—I kicked him in the ass yesterday—really hard!—and this morning I almost crushed his little, whatchamacallums, his little *huevos*, in my hand." Carmen's laughter exploded in the car. "Seriously, Carmen! I could have crippled him."

"Don't worry about it! Subbies love that! They dream about it!"

"But I loved it, too, Carmen! That's what's scary. I got so fucking turned on, I wanted to keep doing it."

"Okay, maybe you should calm down. Just a wee bit."

"Carmen, I know I must sound like a teenage girl after her first makeout date."

"Yeah, kinda."

"And there's a bunch of other stuff I want to tell you, and ask you about. Where are you?"

"At the Muscle Factory. This is our heavy leg day, Hector and me. We're taking turns squatting with two-twenty-five. No way I can match him on weight, but I do more sets and reps. You oughta try heavy squats, by the way, if you want a big bubble booty like mine."

"I'll definitely keep that in mind. So, like, when could we talk?"

"Why don't you come over after work?"

"What time?"

"How about six? I should be finished with my Pilates by then."

"Don't you need time to get home from class?"

"No class today, I'm doing my Pilates at home," Carmen paused, then went on in an exaggerated, snooty voice, "with my personal trainer, la-dee-da."

Kelly laughed out loud. "Okay, Carmen! *Hasta la vista,* baby!"

But, as she clicked off, Kelly felt a twinge of disappointment. She'd been planning to get home as soon as she could after five—the hour at which Chris was to be on his knees by the door—and end the all-day suspense. But actually this was better, she decided. If she kept Chris waiting for her until seven, or even eight, or later, so much the better.

Why not keep him in suspense, awaiting his fate on his knees?

*

For the first half-hour after Kelly left, Chris sat hunched in the breakfast nook, drinking the rest of the coffee and thinking doomsday thoughts.

Then, on a sudden and defiant impulse, he got to his feet, grabbed the peanut butter jar from the cupboard and a big spoon from the drawer and marched into the living room where he settled himself all the way back in the forbidden recliner.

If it was a foregone conclusion .he was going to surrender his manhood as soon as Kelly got home, he might as well enjoy his last few hours of freedom.

But his defiance wasn't done. After several hefty spoonsful of Super Chunky, rather than switching on the TV for the NBA highlights, he decided to get dressed and get the hell out of there for a while. It didn't matter where he looked—at the furniture, the colors and décor, like the fucking crystal ballerinas on the sideboard or the ridiculous needlepoint footstool or the glowering goddess hanging in the bedroom—everything reflected Kelly's style and Kelly's choices. There was no room, not even a tiny corner, he could call his own or that showed any masculine influence.

Maybe once out in the world he could escape this claustrophobic feeling of being held captive in a Testosterone Free Zone.

And yet, en route to the bedroom to get some clothes, Chris had to fight the urge to swerve into the kitchen and tidy up.

"Fuck it!" he yelled at the empty condo, feeling the guilty pleasure of blasphemy, knowing he would never dare say, or even think, such a thing in Kelly's presence.

Moments later, feeling almost like his old self again in a faded blue polo shirt, khaki Dockers and his Skechers slip-ons, Chris regarded himself in Kelly's full-length mirror.

Damn, if he didn't look like a young stud! Why the hell wasn't he? Would a man who looked like that let his wife crush his nuts—and then squeak in falsetto, "Thank you, Goddess"?

Fuck no!

Turning from the accusing mirror, Chris snatched up his condo keys and his wallet, verifying that it held the two twenties and debit card Kelly allowed him to carry, and got the hell out.

This time as he walked along the sidewalk, instead of pitying the men he passed, as he had on his morning errand, Chris found himself envying them.

Unlike me, he thought, they're free, able to go anywhere they want without female permission, to watch sports and drink beer and exercise their masculine likes and dislikes, at least within normal social constraints. He, on the other hand, was an impostor, pretending to be a regular guy as he moved among them. If any of them knew the extent of his pussywhipped existence, and the even more shameful status it would soon be reduced to, they would stare at him like he was an alien. Or, maybe worse, a traitor to his gender.

At the end of the block Chris was brought up short at the open door of the French bakery, enticed by the familiar savory aromas. A counter girl saw him and waved. He waved back but didn't go in.

If he was going to enjoy the condemned man's last meal and stuff his face with verboten pastries, why not walk another block and a half to the Donut Shoppe and buy a bag of glazed buttermilk bars? He hadn't had one of those since... well, since before Kelly. Three fucking years.

Twenty minutes later, Chris was sitting on a bench in a neighborhood park, listening to toddlers scream and squeal under the watchful gaze of stay-at-home moms and Hispanic nannies. There was a crumpled donut sack in his lap, a flaky glaze on his lips, an indigestible lump in his gut, and an empty ache in his soul.

The guilty residue of a three-dollar sugar binge. What a pathetic rebellion!

Once again, at this drunk-in-the-gutter low point, Chris felt the stirrings of his lost manhood. He recalled the conquering thrill he'd felt just last night, preparing to mount Kelly and pound her into orgasmic submission, show her after all these years who was really the boss.

She had thwarted the impulse, but he could still make it happen. He was a fully functioning male animal, almost two inches taller than she and physically stronger. Good-looking, too, as he'd just seen in the mirror. And Kelly was attracted to him in that way, not just to his submissive side. At least she had been once upon a time.

Early on, at college, they'd gone out on some regular dates. He could remember them coming out of a movie in a driving rain and fleeing down the street and sheltering together under an awning. Their faces had met in a gasp of shared excitement that had turned into a surprise kiss. For once her mouth had yielded to his, rather than the other way around, and Chris remembered the growly sound of desire deep in her throat, like a lioness, as he bent her backward in his arms.

What if *that* Chris was waiting for her when she got home, dressed casually as he was now, maybe with two glasses and an open bottle of Malbec on the table? What if, instead of groveling at her feet, he went down on one knee like Galahad or Lancelot and told her he wanted to be her loving husband and champion, not her lowly slave?

And what if he went out and got a real job in his field, finally exercised his artistic talents and ambitions and earned some real money, so Kelly could respect him again and, even more important, so he could respect himself?

He had studied and worked for years to become an artist and designer before being swallowed up by Kelly and her dreams and ambitions. No wonder he was not particularly good at his domestic duties, and why he silently rebelled at the enforced confinement in her condo while she traveled the world and was celebrated for her successes.

With these and many similar thoughts and resolves welling up within, Chris found himself again on his feet, striding more purposefully now as he retraced his steps homeward. It would be a very different kind of reception his wife would find when she returned.

It was just eleven when he reached the block with O'Malley's and saw its doors were open for the lunch-hour trade. Chris hesitated a moment, then stepped inside. It was probably for the last time, he thought, and, anyway, Kelly wasn't due back for several hours.

It looked like he was their first customer. The bartender was changing channels on the big flat screen above the glittery tiers of bottles on the back-bar display, and several waitresses were flitting to and fro in their tight crop tops and short shorts.

Chris took a stool at the near end of the bar. A ponytailed brunette circled around from behind him. "Kitchen's open, want a menu?"

"Thanks, just a beer."

"A Corona with a lime wedge, right?"

"Yes, but how'd you know?"

"I've waited on you before, but usually later in the day. Are you on your lunch break?"

"No, I'm—I'm actually between jobs." Shit! Why did he have to tell her that?

"There's a lot of that going around. What do you do—I mean, when you're actually working?"

"Graphic arts and design."

"Hey, my boyfriend's a graphic artist, or wants to be. He's done some logos and web design and stuff. Right now, though, he's working as a barista. It's a hard field to get into, he says, 'cause everybody and his nephew wants to do it."

"Tell me about it."

Chris remembered her now. She had a perky personality, a short, sexy shape, and her whole face scrunched up and her cheeks dimpled when she smiled, which was often. And she was definitely flirting, he decided, boyfriend or not. He watched her sashay away to get the beer, admiring her saucy bottom in the short shorts.

She returned, set down the frosty bottle with the lime wedge notched on the open rim.

"Thanks. What's your name?"

"You're kidding, right?" She giggled, pointing to the large nametag beside her croptop cleavage.

"Oh, sorry, Leslie. Like duh! I'm Chris." He laughed at himself and wondered what it would be like to have a normal girlfriend like Leslie. A girl who probably hung on your every word on dates, and laughed at even dumb jokes you made. A girl who didn't slap your face for saying the wrong thing. And, yeah, a girl with normal-size tits. Not Super Kelly from the Amazon planet who demanded she be worshipped and obeyed.

Again he admired the show Leslie put on as she pranced away to confer with three other waitresses, all of them cute and competent looking as they wheeled away a moment later on their separate errands, carrying their trays.

The thing was, he thought, they all deserved to be worshipped and obeyed by their boyfriends, they just didn't know it. The prideful way they carried themselves, the magical mischief in their eyes—it was as though, deep down, they knew they were the guardians of the ultimate secrets of life, with the power to create and sustain life in their voluptuous, nurturing bodies.

Women really were a superior race, or gender. How had Kelly put it? "As a male, your position in life is to serve the superior female sex." It was really true. He could see himself as the devoted servant, or slave, of any one of these young women.

What he couldn't see was himself as their boyfriend. Swaggering around, acting cocky and superior. Or even pretending to be their equal, when he clearly was not. It was suddenly starkly obvious to him, his lower status in regard to women.

He'd been an impostor from the moment he'd left the condo, a worthless shell of empty manhood walking down the street all dressed up in his brand-name casual clothes. And the charade had continued when he'd walked in here and plunked down on a stool, just another lunchtime regular ready to flash his macho smile at the serving girls.

The truth was, he was completely hollow inside. Like that poem he'd learned in college:

We are the hollow men
We are the stuffed men
Leaning together...
Filled with straw...

From the first, Kelly Ann Sheffield had seen through him. Seen the vast emptiness and aimlessness inside him. Or maybe she'd done the hollowing-out. It didn't really matter, because the end result was the same. Without a woman to lead him, he was devoid of purpose, with straw for brains.

It was a hell of a realization. But better to know it, he decided, than not to know it and imagine himself something he was not, and maybe never was, but certainly never would be again.

A man.

Leslie drifted back, flashing her scrunched-up, dimpled smile, saw his empty bottle. "Another Corona, Chris?"

"Guess so."

"Is that a yes?"

"Yes, I'd like another."

"You look sad? Can I guess?"

"Go ahead."

She set down a new bottle and, propping her chin on her hands, leveled a sympathetic gaze at him. "Girl trouble?"

"Sort of."

"Don't want to talk about it?"

"It's... kind of awkward. Embarrassing, you might say." He glanced away from her forthright look, suppressing an insane impulse to confess everything to her, including his epiphany just now about female superiority.

"Well, let me know if you want to talk." And she was gone.

All the puzzle pieces were falling into place now. He wouldn't get that graphic arts job, not in a million years. Not because the field was hard to get into, though it was, but because he'd lost the inner fire, the motivation, to forge a career for himself. Any career. He'd traded his life ambitions for a one-in-a-million chance to become Kelly Ann Sheffield's full-time flunky, to help her graduate with honors and launch herself on *her* career. That bargain had been implicit from the beginning, and was becoming more explicit day by day.

"We'll just put your graphics career on the back burner for now, sweetie," he remembered Kelly saying back then. Only he didn't have a back burner. He'd simply abandoned his dreams, and the tiny flame had flickered out forever.

Which explained the fact that in the three years he'd been with Kelly, he hadn't picked up a pencil or a brush, or even played around with his graphics programs on the old MacBook Pro she let him use.

Could he even draw anymore?

When Leslie came back with a fresh bottle, he asked for a pen and began doodling on the cocktail napkin. His hand remembered the movements, but they were mechanical, devoid of any creative impulse. After a moment he realized he was trying to draw Kelly. The result was cartoonish. He was reaching to crumple it when Leslie appeared at his shoulder.

"Why do all guys like ridiculous big boobs? No one has them like that."

"My girlfriend does," Chris said automatically—and with a certain pride.

"Seriously?"

"Yes, seriously."

"And you've got girl trouble? I don't think so! What is she, like a club dancer?"

"She's a sales executive."

"With *those*? You're kidding. Does she make a shitload of money?"

"Yeah, pretty much. Actually, she's never told me how much she makes. I think she invests most of it."

"Wow! You've got it made, Chris! Why do you want to be a graphic artist or anything else? I probably shouldn't have said that, should I? What I mean is—"

"No, you're right. She makes more than enough money for both of us." Chris hesitated, then plunged ahead, yielding to the impulse to reveal himself to this sympathetic girl. "Actually, I lied. She's not my girlfriend, she's my wife. And I'm—I'm not between jobs. I'm her full-time househusband."

"Really?" Leslie stepped around the end of the bar and perched a moment on the stool next to his. She seemed intrigued. "That's great. So, like, do you actually do housework, and stuff like that, or do you pay someone to cook and clean?"

"No, we don't have any servants, though of course she could afford one. She expects me to do all the housework and cooking. That was the deal when we got married. I pledged to serve and obey."

"Hey, I think I saw that on 'Dr. Phil' or one of those. 'Exec Wives and Homemaker Hubbies,' something like that. It kind of makes sense, when you think about it, with so many more girls than guys graduating from college and succeeding in business and stuff."

"Yes, it does," Chris said. "I guess it's long overdue."

"The only thing is," Leslie flashed her dimpled smile, "aren't you supposed to be home scrubbing the floors, instead of in here, talking to me? Not that I want you to leave, don't get me wrong, but I hope you're not getting in trouble. I mean, does she know?"

"No, she doesn't know. I'm, I'm—" Chris' light, bantering tone dissolved mid-sentence, and his next words came out choked with emotion: "I have no business being here. I'm supposed to be cleaning our condo right now, just like you said."

"You're not kidding, are you?"

"No, I'm not," he said quietly.

"Hey, I didn't mean to, you know, make you feel bad."

"It's okay, Leslie. It's what I needed to hear. I need to go home right now."

"Sure, I understand. Look, don't take this the wrong way, Chris, but it's kind of sexy, the way she's got you, you know, by the short hairs. Before you go, do you mind if I bring one of the other girls over for a second to meet you? She's got this boyfriend who's always yelling and bossing her around and expects to be waited on hand and foot. I keep telling her she can do way better. Would you mind talking to her and telling her how your deal works? I think it could really help."

"Sure, that would be fine," Chris said, oddly excited at this prospect of revealing to yet another girl his subservient status as Kelly's househusband.

Raynette, the other girl, was mocha-colored and doll-faced with a shy smile and liquid dark eyes. Chris couldn't imagine anyone yelling at such a gentle, fawnlike creature.

"So I just told Raynette," Leslie said, "that basically your wife is the breadwinner, and you are happy doing all the household chores and, you know, being bossed around a bit, if it's okay to say that?"

"It's not only okay, it's true. She is the boss of me." He laughed nervously. "She deserves to be treated like a queen, and I think a lot of girls do. Maybe all girls. If you ask me, we guys are lucky to live on the same planet with you."

"Hey, I like the sound of that!" Raynette said. "I should have you talk to Mitch, tell him how good he's got it, only the stupid sumbitch wouldn't listen. And I can't get him to pick up anything around our apartment except the TV remote. What's your wife's secret, if you don't mind me asking?"

"No, it's fine. She just—it's pretty much a total thing."

"Does she hold out on you, you know, no sex unless you—"

"Yes, she does, but it's way more than that." He flushed. "I can't even begin to—"

"Does she punish you?"

"That's what I was going to ask," said Leslie. "Like when you go home, if she finds out you were here without permission, and maybe you don't have all your chores done, are you going to be in trouble?"

"Yes," he said. "Yes, I'll be in trouble, and I'll deserve it."

"What will she do? Scold you or, like, you know, in *Fifty Shades*, only in reverse? Does she do stuff like that?"

"I didn't see the movie, but from what I gather, the answer is yes, she does some of that, and she's threatening to do a lot more. But it's not, you know, just a sex game."

"If you say so," Leslie said, "but, you have to admit, it is kind of hot, especially when the woman has the upper hand."

Chris nodded. "Yes, it is. But she does it because I deserve it and need to do better."

Both women nodded, acknowledging his earnest tone, but their eyes were alight with excitement.

"I'd like to ask you a lot more questions," Leslie said, "but maybe that's the wrong thing. Maybe what we should say is, 'Hey, get your butt back to your wife's condo and get busy scrubbing her floors!'"

"Yeah," said Raynette, as both girls giggled at their boldness. "We girls have to stick together! Get your cute little butt in gear!"

"Yes, Ma'am," Chris said. "Or, I guess that should be 'Yes, ladies.'" He stood up abruptly, nodding his head to them in the polite and deferential way that Kelly had taught him.

"But, hey, if your wife ever gets tired of you," added Raynette, "check back with me. I'm thinking seriously about trading Mitch in for a newer model, and I might like to take you for a test drive."

"Why Raynette Jones!" Leslie exclaimed. "You bad girl, you!"

Chris laughed, aware of their following eyes as he made his way out, a bit unsteady on his feet. How many beers had he had? Three, or was it four? Outside in the sun he checked his watch and was shocked to see it was twelve-thirty already. He'd been in O'Malley's an hour and a half!

Drinking too much, and talking way too much. What had caused him to confess his submissive soul to a couple of barmaids?

Because it felt good. And exciting. But also right. Because he no longer felt like a fraud. He felt authentically himself—or had when he'd dropped all pretense and revealed the bottom-line truth about himself to Leslie and Raynette.

You are a submissive, he affirmed to himself, a slave to women. If this was decision day, and it was, then the decision had been made.

When Kelly returned, she would find her husband naked and bowing low to her supreme authority. His pathetic rebellion was over, and his surrender would be unconditional.

*

He walked slowly up the five flights to their condo, but it felt like a descent. He was keyed up, excited, yet at the same time resigned. Or what was that other word Kelly had used? Reconciled. Yes, he was finally reconciled to his fate.

He let himself back in. Home. Her home, of course, not his—but the only place where he truly belonged. Still tipsy, but knowing he was finally on solid ground. He knew what he was, where he was supposed to be and what was expected of him. How many people could say that? He checked the kitchen clock as he gathered up the dirty breakfast dishes. He had four hours to get her place spic-and-span.

His heart lifted. He felt a deep, abiding peace as he turned on the faucet and picked up the sponge. "I belong to you, Kelly," he said aloud, savoring the sacred sound of it. "Always and forever."

But he'd forgotten something. He was wearing clothes!

He switched off the faucet, went straight to the bedroom and undressed. Then stood, staring at his nakedness in the full-length mirror with his cock rising in obedient salute to its absent owner. And heard her mocking voice in his head: "How do you like your new uniform?"

I like it, Goddess, he said to himself. Knowing it was the only acceptable answer.

He looked around. The room was in complete disorder. The bed had to be made and the sheets changed. He stripped off the old ones and carried them with all the dirty clothes from the hamper to the service porch, where he began to separate the whites and colors from her delicates that needed to be carefully hand-washed and hung up to dry.

A moment later he paused with a pair of her lavender satin panties in his hand. Before tossing them onto the pile of lacy underthings, he pressed the panty crotch to his nostrils and inhaled deeply her puissant female scent. The effect was like the first dizzying rush of an intoxicant hitting an addict's bloodstream, and he nearly fainted with the longing that ignited.

By the time he realized what he was doing, it was too late. There was no way he could possibly stop himself. Not after so many maddening weeks of teasing and denial in her hands, and all night suckling at her magnificent breasts.

He grabbed hold of his rigid cock and began to pump himself. *Do it now—you may never have a chance again! She doesn't have to find out!* But, of course, he knew she would—and that he would pay for it later. But he didn't care. Not now.

He stumbled into the living room, threw himself backward into the recliner as he worked himself to the frenzied precipice of desire. Just a few seconds later he was erupting and crying out, hearing himself repeat the abject litany of his devotion to his ruling Goddess, culminating with his longing to belong to her forever and ever.

It was a foreshadowing of the complete surrender soon to come.

CHAPTER NINE ~ DECISION DAY ~ TWO

Kelly switched off the Audi's engine in front of Carmen's apartment complex a few minutes after six, then did her best to switch off her mind—or at least to purge it of work-related thoughts and concerns. This was not an easy task, since, not long after presiding over a highly charged staff meeting that had lasted through lunch, she'd taken the elevator to the top floor to give her own boss a detailed debriefing on her sales trip.

Arn Westrum was a roly-poly gnome of a man, with a sly smile and an IQ off the charts. As with most males, Kelly could read his lustful thoughts—his smile grew especially sly whenever their meetings were one-on-one, she'd noted; but she also knew that the real lust of Arn's life was to make vice president in their parent corporation, and that he'd replace her tomorrow with a toothless hag if the hag could achieve higher sales figures.

Fortunately for Kelly, Arn had found the sales figures she'd presented today nearly as spectacular as the figure she presented standing beside the PowerPoint projection screen in her tight silk blouse and pencil skirt. The particular focus of Arn Westrum's delight was the announcement that she'd landed the convention business of an international association of golf course builders for their new Caribbean resort. It was a major coup, which would add more luster to her rising-star status in the company.

Thank God, Arn did not know she'd risked losing the account by declining the invitation of the association's executive director to spend the night in his penthouse suite.

It was a decision on which Kelly still second-guessed herself, and not for business reasons. Henry Malcolm, though easily old enough to be her father, was one of the sexiest men she'd ever met.

Ah, well! The old lion was still stalking her from afar, still texting her with tempting overtures. "You could always change your mind, *bokkie*," he'd said to her in his clipped South African accent on their last meeting, "and I plan to be in the vicinity when you do."

But Kelly's eventful day wasn't done—not nearly! And the two remaining meetings on her agenda were the ones she'd been looking forward to all day. Carmen, first, and then Christopher, who, by Kelly's reckoning, had been on his knees waiting for her by the door for an hour already! To know that, moment by moment, she was exercising that kind of remote control over her slave husband sent pleasurable tingles coursing through all the right places.

Well, if she could keep a powerful man like Henry Malcolm on the hook, why not her little Christopher for another hour or more? And with this satisfying thought Kelly reached to open the car door.

Then stopped.

A muscular guy in a tanktop and shorts was trotting down the steps from the apartment complex's second floor—Carmen's floor—carrying a big gym bag. A baseball cap hid the shadowy face and, of course, the bald dome, but it had to be Hector, didn't it? Kelly decided to wait till he'd gone, so she could have Carmen all to herself. She watched the macho guy reach the sidewalk, then turn in her direction.

It wasn't Hector, she saw as he came nearer. The nicely muscled arms were tattoo-free, and not cartoonishly large, and the face was Anglo, and a lot better looking than Hector (sorry, Carmen!). *Way better* than good-looking, Kelly realized as he passed right by her car without glancing over. He was a stud on wheels, with a neatly trimmed piratical beard and a kind of Prince Valiant pageboy tucked under his ball cap.

Kelly's eyes shifted to the rear-view mirror, which she adjusted slightly. Yes, indeed, the guy checked out that way, too. In fact, his rear view was so enjoyable that she was disappointed when his one-man parade stopped three cars behind hers at a PT Cruiser. In went the gym bag, and, moments later, the well-worn little car nosed out, U-turned and putted away.

Kelly exhaled mightily and thought, God, I'd love to fuck him! Or, more to the point, and a wee bit unusual for her to admit, be fucked *by* him.

Who was he? she wondered, climbing out in time to see the Cruiser reach the end of the block, then swing right and vanish.

Carmen's personal trainer, that's who!

Of course! Exiting with a gym bag from Carmen's floor at precisely the hour she said she'd be done with her Pilates class.

Carmen Gallegos, you naughty, naughty girl! And what about Hector?

Of course, Kelly was making all kinds of wild assumptions and leaping to all kinds of kinky conclusions, but something told her she was right on all counts. And she couldn't wait to find out for sure.

Halfway up those same steps, Kelly had another thought: Maybe she should take Pilates, too!

*

Chris couldn't remember who or what he'd been fleeing in his dream when a sudden drumming of actual footsteps in the stairwell jolted him awake.

Kelly—coming fast!

He jackknifed up and out of the recliner and frantically checked the time on his cell phone.

Holy shit! It was eleven minutes after five!

He rushed across the room, then flung himself forward in a knee-slide, praying he'd reach the door before it opened. He came to rest on the rag-rug welcome mat and, with his heart thumping away, bent his torso all the way forward to display his total submission.

He'd made it, thank God!

What an idiot he'd been! Not just for jerking off, but actually falling asleep afterward in the recliner, then oversleeping again, just like the night her plane was delayed! If Kelly had come in and found him like that—instead of like this, obediently cowering in place—she'd have killed him. Well, for sure booted him out the door.

She still might, he realized. He could feel the dried cum all over his belly and crotch. And her condo was a disaster—nothing had been picked up since, basically, his big cleanup the day before. There were dirty dishes in the kitchen, her bed was stripped of all linens, there were pillows on the floor, dirty clothes strewn all over the service porch.

She'd definitely kick him and slap him around—she had every

right to. But at least, thank God, he was in place at the required time. He'd suffer the consequences, whatever they were.

But the door didn't open. Instead, the pounding footfalls went on echoing up the stairwell toward the floor above.

A reprieve! Now, at least, he had time for a quick cleanup, maybe even a fast shower.

Or did he?

Did he dare leave his designated spot by the door? Even to clean the kitchen, even for a frantic one-minute whirlwind tour, picking up and putting away, forget about making the bed?

No, he didn't dare! What if Kelly deliberately came up the stairs quietly, to test him, then threw the door open—and he wasn't right there at her feet?

The thought chilled him. No matter what terrible sins he'd committed, how many new rules he'd violated, he had to be in his place, his nose in the rag rug and his naked ass exposed, awaiting the return of his goddess.

For how long?

As long as it takes, came the obvious answer.

*

Since wearing even a watch was now forbidden him, Chris had no way of knowing how long he remained crouched there awkwardly by the door. But after only a few minutes his thighs and knees and hips and ankles all began to ache, and the urge to alter his position became overpowering.

And yet, clenching his teeth, he remained in place, making only tiny, fractional adjustments to relieve the unremitting pain. Only later was he able to calculate that his Goddess had kept him waiting at least two and a half hours.

What kept him there? Love and devotion? Possibly. Temporary insanity? Almost certainly. But more than anything, he knew, it was fear. Fear of the She-Goddess who had conquered his mind, his emotions, his very soul.

Despite all of that, finally he did reach his breaking point—then went a little ways beyond it. He began to count, promising himself that, upon reaching a hundred, he would collapse full-length on the floor. Only by imagining the exquisite relief that would soon be his was he able to endure those additional excruciating seconds— seconds that were to spell the difference between failure and success.

For, as his desperate count reached a hundred, and then, in a final, frenzied extension, into the hundred-and-thirties, he heard approaching steps—unmistakably hers this time. He abandoned his count as he followed her upward progress from the stairs to the landing, the footsteps growing louder, coming closer.

Thank God! With eyes clamped tight and face pressed into the rug, Chris heard the door opening, felt the kiss of outside air on his nakedness, heard the solid thunk of her briefcase being set down, then the door closing.

"Hello, Slaveboy," she said huskily. The tip of her shoe poked his cheek, then wedged itself under his mouth and nose. He began kissing it, and then began sobbing. He couldn't help himself.

"Well, I guess I have my answer. My sweet boy. My sweet, sweet boy."

"Welcome home, Goddess," he said when he was able.

"I like the sound of that, Christopher. And I see that you're nice and hard for your Goddess. Now lift your head so you can lick the bottom of my shoe."

Kelly flexed her foot, exposing the herringbone grid on the bottom of her Nike trainer, then pushed it toward his face. Chris started licking the hard-rubber surface.

"Are you enjoying yourself down there, slave? You can answer between licks."

"Yes, Goddess Kelly."

"But don't you think it's perverted and degrading?"

"Yes, Goddess."

"But it feels right, doesn't it?"

"Yes, Goddess, it does."

"Because it shows your proper place in our relationship."

"Yes, Goddess."

"What is your place, slave?"

"At your feet, my Goddess."

"And never forget it. Now untie my shoe and slip it off."

Chris complied, doing it by feel so he could maintain his facedown position.

"Now my sock." He pulled it off and began to kiss and lick her toes through the nylon mesh of her pantyhose, savoring the salty tang and sweaty aroma—until she nudged his face away.

"That's enough. Now roll your face toward me, but keep your

cheek on the floor."

Chris did as told, and was rewarded when she stepped on the side of his face with her bare foot, as if claiming him for her own.

"Do you like that, slave? When I step on your face?"

"Yes, Goddess." And it was true, God help him. He really did!

"How about when I do this?" She pressed her foot down much harder.

"Yes, Goddess!" he gasped.

Kelly fought a wicked impulse to step up and balance all her weight on the one foot, but thought better of it. Christopher might be only a slave, but he was, after all, *her* slave, and she needed to take good care of her property.

"Whether you like it or not," she said, estimating that only about half her weight was now pressing down on him, "you have to suffer it for me anyway, isn't that so, Slaveboy?"

"Yes, Goddess, it is."

She stepped off him. Except for the heaving of his chest as he gulped for air, he remained still, not daring to move a muscle without permission, which pleased her very much.

"At first," Carmen had warned, "all this will seem like just a kinky little game you're playing together. But pretty soon, for both of you, it becomes real, a lifestyle, the way you live. When that happens—and you need to be prepared for this, Kelly girl—you won't be able to see Chris as your husband anymore or even your lover. He'll really and truly be your slave."

It was already beginning to happen, Kelly realized. Despite her fond, possessive feelings for Christopher, she couldn't help viewing him with increasing disdain. He was a male creature, of course, but not a man anymore, not a real man. Would Henry Malcolm, say, or that hunky Pilates guy cringe and cower at her feet, let himself be slapped and kicked around like a cur?

Of course not!

"But subbies, like my Hector or your Chris," Carmen had said, "they love all that stuff, they can't get enough of it. We're only helping them achieve their real destiny as our inferior, pussywhipped slaves. And doing that is not only a real turn-on, it's incredibly addictive, you'll see!"

There was an additional benefit Kelly could share with her mentor. Coming home to a naked, groveling male pet, as she was finding out, could be the perfect stress-reliever after a grueling day in the executive jungle.

She turned her attention back to Chris. "That was a bit extreme, little slave, but in addition to learning your place at my feet, I'm teaching you another important lesson. Shall I tell you what it is?"

"Yes, Goddess, please."

"How polite! I like that, Christopher. I'm teaching you to fear my power over you, and my willingness to use it. Can you guess why that's important for you?"

"So I'll always obey you, Goddess?"

"Very good!" Kelly was extremely impressed with his answer. "I will expect instant obedience from you at all times, and that means without thinking. It won't be easy, but really, that's all you have to worry about. You don't have to think about getting a job or a career—we're way beyond that now. You won't have to decide what clothes to wear, because you won't be wearing any. You don't have to worry about how your favorite sports team is doing. You won't be watching TV either. And you certainly don't have to trouble your little mind about politics or world events. You'll vote the way I tell you to, just as you did last election. Pleasing me and obeying me—that's your entire world from now on, Christopher. Won't that simplify things—just the way I've simplified your conversation by reducing it to 'yes, Goddess,' or 'no, Goddess.' Hmm?"

"Yes, Goddess. But what if—"

Kelly stopped his mouth with the ball of her foot, annoyed by his attempt to talk further. "You don't have permission to speak now. I've had a bitch of a day, and I want to put my feet up and have a glass of wine and check my messages while you massage my feet and suck my toes. Take off my other shoe and sock and then crawl into the kitchen and pour me a glass of wine—some cabernet, I think—and bring it to me in the recliner. Got that?"

She unsealed his mouth. "Yes, my Goddess."

Kelly looked down, extremely pleased with the rapid progress of Christopher's enslavement. As soon as he'd removed her remaining shoe and sock, she used her foot to nudge him away on his errand, then turned toward her favorite recliner.

That's when everything came crashing down.

On the floor in front of the big chair she'd glimpsed something totally out of place, purple and shiny, a scrap of fabric. As she walked slowly and deliberately toward it, the scrap resolved itself into a discarded pair of panties. *Her* panties, obviously.

Out of the corner of her eye she saw Chris halt on his knees, watching her.

"Goddess, I didn't—" he began to stammer.

"Shut up!"

She bent and plucked her satin panties off the floor, her fingers finding the sticky, wet spot even before she saw the telltale stains. But that wasn't the only thing wrong. A single sweeping glance now revealed a breakfast table littered with dirty dishes and cups and a crumpled napkin, a half-and-half carton left out on the kitchen counter.

Kelly didn't use cream with her coffee, only Chris did. But not anymore.

She swung around. He was kneeling right beside her, his face the picture of guilt, like a dog who has chewed up a favorite pair of slippers.

"Stand up, slave."

When he stood fully exposed before her, Kelly bent to examine the snail-track residue of semen on his chest and stomach and glistening in his pubic hair. His erection was not as vertical as usual, she noted, and his balls seemed to sag a bit more than they had this morning. She took his scrotum in her fist and gave a sharp downward tug that made him wince. Finally she palpated his testicles to further confirm what was already patently obvious. And, indeed, they felt a tad light.

Chris had continued to flinch during this examination, but retained his three-quarters salute. "I'm so sorry, Goddess! I–I just—" Chris broke off, seeing Kelly's right knee lifting off the floor.

"No, please, Goddess, don't!"

But it was too late. Her lower leg whipped forward in a pendulum kick, her foot catching Chris right in the scrotum. He screamed and dropped to the floor, groaning as he grabbed his knees and rolled away from her.

"Haven't you forgotten something, slave? Remember this morning? What did I teach you to say after I gave your balls a good squeeze?"

"Thank you, Goddess!" he gasped.

"That's right, please remember next time. And, rest assured, there will be a next time."

She straddled his tightly curled form, waiting until he looked up fearfully before continuing: "I come home from an extremely hard day at the office to find that you've ejaculated without my permission, and left my home in a complete shambles, doing absolutely no housework, having prepared nothing for my dinner! You had all day, Christopher, and you did nothing but jerk off! Tell me, what do you think your punishment should be?"

"You're absolutely right, goddess, I deserved that kick, and I—"

"Shut up, Christopher! You can't actually think that was your punishment? A barefoot kick? No, sweetie, that was simply to get your attention—like this." She administered a swift kick to his right butt cheek. "Better get used to it. That's one reason I'm keeping you naked, so every part of you will be accessible to me at all times. Now get up on your knees and face me."

"I can't, Goddess," he groaned. "Please, just give me a minute."

"Do as I say or I'll kick you again! Your nuts are still exposed, you know. I can see them peeking out."

Still moaning, Chris struggled to his knees. His erection, Kelly saw, had shriveled to nothingness, and his faltering gaze did not quite meet hers. An altogether pitiful excuse for a man, she thought, and entirely in her power.

With languid grace, she seated herself in the recliner, tilting all the way back to regard him through the frame of her extended bare feet. "The truth is, Christopher, I didn't want to get into this now, the whole matter of your punishment. There are several other things I intended to deal with first, all of which I assure you would be much less unpleasant for you. But you've forced my hand with your reckless and unforgivable behavior."

"I'm sorry, Goddess."

"Not as sorry as you soon will be. Now I will give you the good news. You will not be whipped, or caned, or flogged, because I don't have any of those useful implements..." she smiled wickedly before adding, "at least not yet. We're going to have to make do with what's already on hand, so to speak. Perhaps a spatula or a wooden kitchen spoon, what do you think?"

Kelly was thinking out loud and enjoying every aspect of this, especially watching the unmistakable flickers of fear in Christopher's eyes—or was it terror? "Of course, there's always milady's hairbrush, but I don't think I have one with the right kind of heft. What about a ping-pong paddle? Do we have one of those in the spare room?"

"I don't think so, Goddess."

"No, neither do I."

Suddenly, Kelly knew precisely what implement she was going to use to initiate her slave's virgin ass. She instructed him where to go and what to bring back—on his knees, both ways—then, like a potentate, dismissed him with a handclap and watched him crawl off, his scrotal sac swinging in rear-view like some barnyard animal's.

Then, as the butterflies of excitement began swarming in her tummy, she grabbed her cell phone and, taking a quick photo, sent it to Carmen with a funny caption, and got back an instant reply—*"His ass is SO cute!!!! You go, Kelly girl!!!!"*—followed by two lines of smiley faces.

*

Chris dragged himself away, feeling like a beaten dog. He knew he deserved punishment for what he'd done, and what he'd failed to do, as they said in church. He'd freely admitted that, hadn't he? But nobody deserved this kind of cruel treatment!

And, incredibly, from what she'd just said, his real punishment was just beginning!

He couldn't run away, he'd been all through that today. He did want to be her slave, despite the cruelty, despite the crippling ache in his testicles where she'd just kicked him. He just had to get through this somehow, and then it would be over. He pictured snuggling his face into her magnificent breasts, or between her luscious thighs as he crawled into the guest bedroom in quest of the implement she wanted.

Kelly had converted the room into her home gym, so Chris had to weave his way around the big elliptical machine and between the treadmill and adjustable combo bench to the wall-to-wall closet.

Inside, just where she'd said, he spotted the big, soft-sided YSL boatbag she'd taken to the Bahamas last winter when she'd gone sailing on somebody's fancy yacht. He unzipped it, rummaged through the workout gear till he touched hard leather. He felt a cold shiver of fear as he pulled it out.

The heavy-duty leather weightlifter's belt was tightly coiled, at least four- or five inches wide and maybe a half-inch thick with a big steel buckle. Chris' heartbeat sped up, and he felt distinctly lightheaded.

She couldn't really mean to use this thing on him, could she?

"What's the matter?" Kelly called from the next room. "Can't you find it? Isn't it where I said?"

"Yes, Goddess," he said, trying to sound calm. "I have it."

"Then bring it here! Hurry, I want to punish you now!"

Against all sense and reason, Chris did exactly as she'd bidden. There was no point in telling himself this was all a crazy dream. It was fucking real—and about to get even realer, if there was such a word.

From the recliner, Kelly watched Christopher lurch toward her on all fours, head hung in defeat, the heavy belt dragging from one hand. He really is my slave, she realized with an erotic thrill. Putting a collar on him would only make it official.

She sat forward and had Chris bow low, offering her the belt in his extended arms. She took it, undid the buckle and let the heavy leather uncoil in her hands to its full serpentine length.

No wonder he's so scared, she thought. It was a lot thicker and stiffer than the punishment strap Carmen had shown her earlier that evening. So thick that, swinging it by the buckle end, she'd need both hands to control it. Maybe she should call Carmen and check before using it on Chris?

No, she thought. I can do this. I'll just be careful.

CHAPTER TEN ~ FIRST PUNISHMENT

Kelly had positioned Chris over the back of the loveseat, bare feet on the carpet, head upside down on the seat cushion, naked ass in the air. She spoke now almost apologetically:

"We've tried everything else, and nothing has worked. Your apologies, your tears, your vows and promises to do better, they mean nothing. When I go off to work and leave you alone, you revert to your old ways. You shirk your chores. You forget your place and all the rest of it, over and over, *ad nauseum.*"

Kelly had already made him confess to everything he'd done that day, and he'd given it all up in a rush of humiliating detail—from binging on peanut butter and buttermilk bars to the three beers at O'Malleys, then telling the barmaids about his slave-husband status before stumbling home half-drunk, and concluding with his unauthorized and shameful masturbation into her soiled panties before falling asleep.

But Chris understood that, while all had been confessed, nothing had been forgiven. Everything he'd told her was stored away as information that could and would be used against him later.

"Now before we start, I'm going to give you one last chance to defy me. What do you say, sweetie? Don't you want to rise up and thump your chest and assert your male prerogatives, whatever those might be?"

"No, Goddess."

"So, you're going to be a complete pushover once again?"

"Yes, Goddess."

"Really, Christopher, did you even think about it? If you stood up to me, even once, I might actually learn to respect you as a man. I mean, you are a handsome, studly-looking guy, if a girl didn't know better. Hmm? What do you think about that?"

"I can't think right now," Chris said honestly.

"Oh, dear, I'm afraid I've confused your poor little male brain with too many options. Have I done that?"

"Yes, Goddess." It was true. Awaiting his strapping, unable to see her with his head upside down in the loveseat, Chris was already in complete panic mode, and her tricky little speech only made his brain spin faster out of control. All he knew for sure was that, no matter the outcome, he couldn't stand up to her—that was the bottom line. Submission to Kelly had become his default setting.

"So, then, you accept that I own you, body and soul, and that I have the right to punish you in any way I see fit at any time?"

"Yes, Goddess Kelly, I do."

"Very good. Then prepare yourself to surrender totally to my female authority and receive your punishment. Do not move a muscle until I say you can."

Christopher heard the faint rustle of her skirt over her nylons, her deep breathing. He dared one quick peek, backward and upward, and, with a stab of fear, glimpsed the fearsome, wide leather belt suspended tongue-down from her right hand.

Chris knew the muscled power of Kelly's physique. He had been allowed to watch and admire her working out—lifting dumbbells, swinging kettlebells, pulling cables. And he also knew the steely determination of her will.

He prayed silently now for mercy at her hands and for the endurance to get through what was about to come.

*

Like a lioness in a small cage, Kelly paced to and fro slowly, making a final inspection of her property, especially Christopher's perky little virgin ass, which she was about to use for target practice.

Several times in the last few minutes she'd wondered if she could really go through with this. But her own excited breathing told her she needn't have doubted her resolve. Nothing could stop her now.

Chris heard the belt swish suddenly through the air and flinched, but there was no impact. *She's taking a practice swing, just like a batter in the on-deck circle.* The second swish did connect, causing him to cry out. But it was just a feint, a light tap.

Kelly exploded with girlish laughter at his overreaction.

A third contact, against one butt cheek, was another light touch. Again Christopher, with every muscle tensed, gasped as it landed, eliciting more laughter.

She was teasing him, but she was nervous, too. *Maybe she can't go through with it!*

Then the first real blow struck—and the blinding pain of it shocked Chris' mind as well as his body. He couldn't believe that the love of his life had just done that to him, and he wanted desperately to jump up and run away. "No, Goddess Kelly, please!" he pleaded, turning his head but unable to see her in his awkward head-down position. "I can't do this! I change my mind!"

"It's too late for that, Christopher," she said sternly, "and this won't do at all. You can't scream like that or the neighbors will be pounding on the door."

"I—I didn't know I screamed, Goddess."

"My God, Christopher, you sounded like you were auditioning for a slasher film! I didn't strike you *that* hard. Just remain absolutely still while I take off my pantyhose and stuff them into your mouth. That should quiet you down."

With his backside aflame, Chris heard the slithery sound of her nylon tights sliding down her legs, then, a moment later, her hands were on his face.

"Mouth open, slave." He obeyed and had it stuffed full, almost to gagging, with a tightly rolled wad of pantyhose. Next the nylon legs were wrapped twice around the lower half of his head, pulled tight and knotted at the nape of his neck.

"Now, slave, try to scream."

Chris tried, but emitted only a faint, muffled grunt.

"Much better. Okay, you have my permission to scream all you want now."

And scream he did, for all he was worth, and several times came very near to running out the door, naked and in pantyhose bondage. Only by screaming silently and clutching the sofa cushion with a death grip did he manage to stay where he was, while praying ceaselessly for her to stop. But the leather strap was merciless, blow after paralyzing blow resounding in the room like an artillery barrage. The brutality he was suffering at her hands continued to shock him, until, finally, he could take no more. Before the next blow could land, he pushed himself backward and threw himself prostrate at her feet, crying out his muted entreaties for mercy.

With the rhythmic reports of leather on flesh still echoing in her mind, Kelly looked down at this broken, red-blotched thing with more annoyance than compassion. How dare he disobey her command to remain in place! What right did he have to ask for his suffering to be over?

None, whatsoever. She, and she alone, would decide that.

She raised the heavy belt, intending to bring it down on his naked ass, already deeply imprinted with fiery red strokes and patches.

Instead, as her arms reached their apex, she let go the belt and stepped back as it clattered to the floor. Then she turned, chest heaving, one hand braced against the loveseat while her other slid beneath the waistband of her panties and down into slippery wetness. In a few frantic seconds, she unleashed the massive orgasm that had been slowly building and gathering all evening.

Dear Lord, she had no fucking idea it would be like this! She'd lost all track of time, of how many strokes she'd delivered, or how fierce they'd been.

Lucky for Christopher, and for her, that he'd thrown himself at her feet when he did. Because the harder she'd struck him, the more powerful she'd felt and the more excited she'd become.

Affectionately now, as she floated down from her climax, Kelly placed one bare foot on the back of Christopher's head, bearing down enough to push his face into the carpet. She was pleased that he had heard her orgiastic cries. He would certainly know the frightening implications of that—his Goddess got off on beating his ass!

It was only then, glancing down, that Kelly noticed the tremors in Christopher's head and shoulders and picked up the suppressed sounds of sobbing through his nylon gag.

"Are you all right, slave?" Kelly heard herself say, with more tenderness than she actually felt.

Christopher turned a ruined face to her, afflicted, tear-filled eyes above his ridiculous pantyhose gag. Then, seeing her naked foot slide off his head, he slithered toward it and began kissing it—or trying to, comically, through his gag—but more passionately, Kelly thought, than he'd ever done before. Was this out of simple gratitude that she'd granted him mercy? Or merely to show his complete acceptance of her supreme authority?

Whatever it was, she liked it. It solidified his new status as her complete underling.

She did wonder if he'd experienced that submissive chemical high that Carmen had mentioned. Kelly hoped so, for his sake, but didn't really care one way or the other. Like it or not, from now on, he'd be submitting to regular punishment at her hands.

As for Christopher's injuries, the truth was Kelly felt a certain pride in having marked her property so severely. He wasn't bleeding, thank God, but he'd be rainbowed with bruises for days and days, she thought, and probably be unable to sit down.

But, after all, a slave didn't need to sit, did he?

*

Chris stood naked, facing a blank wall of the dining room while using his nose to keep a penny trapped against the flat surface. With his back to the room, he couldn't see Kelly, of course, but she was near enough that he could hear her fingers tapping her iPad screen from time to time. Which meant she would hear the coin if it dropped and clattered on the hardwood floor; in which case, she had promised, he would be severely punished—yes, even on top of his just-inflicted injuries.

It was called "corner time," Kelly had explained, a favorite form of humiliation visited upon wayward boys by generations of no-nonsense schoolmarms. The punishment sometimes involved a stool placed in a corner and a dunce cap placed on the boy's head. Holding a penny in place with one's nose was a modern refinement, and an extremely effective way of enforcing the rule that the miscreant remain motionless for the duration.

What that duration would be for him, Chris had no idea. He was to stand there perfectly motionless, pressing the penny flat to the wall, until his Goddess wife released him, whether that was five minutes or all night. But he need not worry, she assured him, he would have ample time to meditate on why he had been so severely punished and to resolve himself to be a better slave to her in future. "And," she had added with special emphasis, "you can expect to receive corner time not only after every punishment session, but any other time I think it could be useful in your training."

Actually, Christopher had understood little of this. Oh, he'd heard the words and phrases being directed at him by Goddess Kelly, but he'd been in too much shock and distress from his beating to comprehend much of anything, even the simplest concepts. Not only were his physical resources exhausted, but his thought processes, too, seemed impaired. When she'd finally helped him to his feet and removed his pantyhose gag, he'd been barely able to speak. Only the fact that his responses were limited to "Yes, Goddess" and "No, Goddess" had saved him from total incoherence.

And now, perhaps a quarter-hour into his corner time, just remaining on his feet had become a second-by-second ordeal, and only his terror of additional punishment enabled him to keep the coin from sliding down the wall.

But worse than the fiery pain up and down his back and buttocks and legs, and the adrenal exhaustion from combating it, and the confusion of his mind, worse even than the humiliation of his ridiculous position, was the knowledge that this would be his life from now on.

A shameful life that would make his parents sick.

Yet Chris could find no spark within him to protest his fate, or this latest instance of Kelly's playful cruelty. The little mutiny he had staged this morning—strutting around the neighborhood, buying doughnuts and going to O'Malleys—had been just a last pathetic fling, pretending to be something he was not, like all those other guys on the street who got to wear clothes and have spending money and follow sports and have opinions.

After tonight, Chris knew, he'd never again be able to look another man in the eye as an equal. Or, even worse, look himself in the mirror without an abiding shame for what he'd become.

Before striking the first blow, Kelly had offered a last chance for him to back out. She was mocking him, of course, but that really had been his last chance, he realized now. For his only impulse now, and it was almost overwhelming, was not to flee or protest, but to throw himself once again at her feet, to get as low as he possibly could to the floor, to show her once and for all his absolute surrender to her power and authority.

*

Kelly put down her iPad and clapped her hands. "Time, slave," she called. "Let the coin go and crawl here to my feet. You may kiss them."

At this sudden reprieve, Chris simply collapsed, straight down in a heap like a puppet whose strings had been cut. Kelly had to stifle a laugh at the comic aspect, reminding herself that, after all, he must be truly exhausted from his punishment and the emotional strain he'd been under all day.

But this day wasn't done, not for either of them. Several items remained on her checklist, and Kelly was not about to let them slide.

CHAPTER ELEVEN ~ A SPECIAL PRESENT ~ ONE

Seeing that Christopher was too exhausted to kneel up before her, Kelly sat forward in the recliner and placed her bare feet on the floor. Chris needed no further prompting and began immediately to kiss and lick them, all the while weeping quietly.

He really was in a state, she realized.

She uncapped her water bottle and set it beside his head. "I want you to stop what you're doing, slave, and drink some of this, as much as you can. I think you may be dehydrated. And have you eaten anything besides those frightful doughnuts this morning, or whatever they were?"

"No, Goddess."

"Well, we'll see about getting some actual food into you later. I'm hungry, too, by the way. But right now I want you to drink."

Chris had to struggle a bit, she saw, just to raise his head high enough to tip the water bottle into his mouth. Seeing this, and realizing her slave's total dependence on her, Kelly was filled again with possessive affection, and it occurred to her that she ought to get him a dog bowl that she could fill with water for times such as these, say, after harsh punishment sessions or long corner times. Then he could drink his fill while keeping his head down, where it truly belonged, at her feet.

But Christopher had managed to empty a third of the bottle, she was pleased to see now, and was looking up at her gratefully, with fresh tears in his eyes and more wetness leaking from the corner of his mouth. She reached down and patted his head.

"Do you have the strength to rise up on your knees now, slave? Here, put a hand on my knee, it'll help you steady yourself."

When he was kneeling up before her, Kelly leaned forward and, taking him by both ears, planted a light kiss on his forehead.

"There! I've been wanting to do that ever since I saw Snow White do it to Dopey! You're not quite that cute, sweetie, but almost. And I know you were trying to be very brave for your Goddess tonight, even though you disobeyed me by leaving your position over the loveseat before I was finished with you. But I want you to know you're not going to be punished extra for that because... well, because I'm in a forgiving mood... and perhaps I did get a little carried away. It was a first time for both of us, wasn't it, little slave? The first of many. And we'll both get better in our respective roles, I assure you. But I think you should really thank your Goddess for overlooking your willful disobedience, don't you?"

Chris bowed his head to her. "Yes, my Goddess, thank you."

"You're forgiven, slave, but you're never to do that again! You'll take your punishment until I say it's over!" She reached out and, cupping his chin, tilted his face back upward. Once again, Christopher's eyes were filled with tears; but, shining through, was a look of profound wonder and adoration.

Kelly was deeply affected by this, and by a new bond of intimacy she felt growing between them, an intimacy enhanced, she was certain, by his complete physical surrender to her authority, and, yes, to her cruelty.

Overcome by a maternal urge, Kelly unbuttoned her silk blouse; then, as her slave watched avidly, she bared her left shoulder and tugged down her bra strap and cup, spilling out the immense, quivering globe, and held it out for him.

"Here, sweetie, put this in your mouth and nurse, it will help calm you down."

A delicious tingle spread throughout Kelly's body as she watched her slave slip into his infantile bliss state on her nipple. He was not only being comforted, she thought, but actually nourished in some mystical way. She began to detect renewed strength in the fingers clutching her breast, in his greedily sucking mouth, and in the low purr of contentment deep in his throat.

Then she glanced down and saw his jutting hard-on—at nearly full staff—another sign of her restorative powers. But even as she admired its size and shape, she found herself wondering if Henry Malcolm would have a larger cock. Kelly was pretty sure he would. Not only was he a man's man, but his hands were much larger than Christopher's, if there was any truth to that correlation.

She was distracted from these pleasant speculations by her slave, whose squeezing fingers and insistent sucking were, frankly, becoming a bit bothersome. So, impatient to move things along, she pushed his face away from her breast. Chris was zoned out, still fixated on her erect nipple with a glazed, cross-eyed stare. Kelly slapped him lightly, and then heavily, before she finally got him to focus properly.

"That's all you're going to get for now, slave," she said, recupping her left tit and rebuttoning her blouse. "There are several things I need to go over with you before I send you off to bed. You're exhausted, I know. But try and pay attention so I won't have to keep slapping you.

"We need to talk about our new arrangement in a little more detail. I gave you some new rules this morning, but I only had time for three or four. I want you to start a notebook to keep track of them as we go along. Eventually there'll be many pages, and you'll be responsible for knowing them all, and of course obeying them. But here are just a couple more for now. Are you ready?"

"Yes, my Goddess." He was trying to look alert, she could tell, but his underlying expression was one of almost comical bewilderment.

"Don't worry, you don't have to take notes now, these are easy. Can you guess what they deal with?"

"Punishment, Goddess?"

Kelly gave a low chuckle. "Well, I can see why that would be uppermost in your little mind. And punishment sessions will certainly be a regular part of your life. But, if you keep my home spotless, take excellent care of my clothes and serve appetizing and nutritious meals on time and so on, I don't envision beating you quite so severely, at least not for minor lapses. Of course, I will inspect your work closely, much more thoroughly than I did the night I came home from my trip, and your level of service will be monitored and evaluated constantly. But if you are totally obedient to me, and perform satisfactorily, you may get only what are called reminder punishments, just to remind you of your place.

"But there are a few other things I do want to mention. The first one has to do with the furniture. Remember a night or so ago when I told you to stay off the recliners?"

"Yes, Goddess, I remember."

"Well, that applies from now on, to all the furniture. After tonight, I don't think you'll be able to sit down for awhile anyway, so that should help you get used to this new rule. You're not to sit on anything, Chris, with the exception of the toilet—and you're not to sit on my personal throne anymore either. The master bathroom is for my exclusive use. You're to keep it clean, of course, but you'll use the little guest bathroom and keep your toiletries there, out of sight in the cabinet under the sink."

"Please, Goddess, may I ask a question?"

"Go ahead, but this had better be the last interruption."

"I'm sorry, Goddess, but what if—what if I need to sit down, I mean, to rest, maybe just for a minute?"

"You do altogether too much resting as it is, Christopher. But if you absolutely have to sit, you'll sit on the floor, as befits your station. Surely that's obvious. And the rule applies whether I'm here or not. Unfortunately, you've proven yourself completely untrustworthy in my absence, so that's a problem I'm going to have to solve. But I'm hoping that, after tonight, you'll think twice about disobeying any of my rules. Am I right in this?"

"Yes, Goddess," Chris said meekly.

"I hope so for your sake. But consider yourself warned, if I ever find out that you've been sitting on the furniture or watching television, or wearing clothes or disregarding any of my rules—you will be a very sorry young man. I think you've seen tonight the kind of serious consequences you can expect to suffer at my hands."

"Yes, Goddess, I have."

"Good. Now, let's see, there was something else about furniture I wanted to mention. Oh, yes. My bed. You won't be sleeping in it. For tonight, you can sleep on the floor in my sleeping bag—the Eddie Bauer one in the guest room closet."

"You mean the rule is just for tonight, right?"

"No, the rule is every night from now on. The 'tonight' part refers only to using my sleeping bag, because really, it's much too good for a slave. Tomorrow I'll find something more appropriate."

Chris felt himself spiraling down into despair as he recalled all those blissful nights cuddled up to the most incredible girl in the world, and especially last night, suckling at her glorious bosom. "But, Goddess, you—I mean, you can't really—"

His sputtering protest was cut short with a stinging slap. "How dare you presume to tell me what I can and cannot do! A lowly slave doesn't get to sleep with the Goddess who owns him! The idea is absurd! And if you question me again, I'll put you in my closet tonight and close the doors on you. In fact, I may do that anyway. Is that clear, slave?"

"Yes, Goddess Kelly. I'm so sorry!"

"There are other rules we'll need to discuss, but I'll save them for another time. Because I want to talk to you about—well, about sex. And sexual freedom—my freedom, obviously, since you don't have any. Do you, slave?" She punctuated the question by reaching down for a quick, hard squeeze of his testicles, causing Chris to convulse and gasp for air.

"No, Goddess," he was finally able to answer, "I don't!"

"Unless your version of sexual freedom is jerking off whenever I'm out of sight."

"I'm so sorry about that! Goddess! You know I am!"

"So you say, but the problem hasn't been solved, even though you've finally been punished for it. So now we're going to try something else. I'd like you to stand up now, slave. Are you able to do that?"

"Nodding, Chris got to his feet with only a few wobbles.

Kelly looked him up and down. "You know, Christopher, you really have a very nice body. But it's not as manly as I'd like. You could use much larger muscles." She fingered his modest biceps, then patted his boyish pectorals. "But, then, you're not exactly a macho guy, are you?"

Chris lowered his gaze. "No, Goddess. I'm not."

"Too bad for you, I guess, huh? Because sometimes, you know, a girl wants a macho guy."

He glanced sharply up at this. Was he wondering if she had someone specific in mind? If so, she would fan his suspicions a little and deal a further blow to his male pride:

"Did I ever tell you about the other guy at that college dance class who I almost picked up instead of you?"

"I think you mentioned him once."

"Well, did I mention he was a real stud? Except he was even more bashful than you, if that's possible. He was taller, too, maybe six-three or six-four. And when we danced close—I have to confess, I kept shoving my tits into him, a lot more than I did with you—he got so excited that, I swear, I could see the outline of what looked like a horsecock stuffed down one pantleg. I mean, he was really, really big, way bigger than you. And now, thinking back, I'm wondering if he might not have been better for me, and maybe wishing I'd picked him. God, I almost did!"

Kelly watched with satisfaction the hurtful effects of her words on Christopher. He'd reacted with visible pain to each inflammatory detail. She feigned sympathy:

"Have I hurt your feelings, sweetie?"

"Kell—I mean Goddess Kelly, you—you said you weren't looking for a stud, remember? You told me you wanted someone who'd—who'd follow your lead in all things and never initiate, who'd be completely—you know, passive."

"I know, I know." Kelly spoke soothingly, idly reaching down to stroke his now-drooping penis, quickly stiffening it to respectability. "But sometimes, Christopher, a girl wants what she doesn't think she wants. Maybe just for a change. More muscles and, you know, a bigger dick?" She encircled his now rigid shaft with thumb and forefinger, then enlarged the circle's diameter and slid it out several inches past the empurpled tip of his glans, illustrating the sort of thickness and length she had in mind. "A real man, not a boy-man. You know, one of those three-ball guys who doesn't pee in his pants every time a girl raises her voice."

Christopher looked to be in a complete tailspin now. But she was mindful of Carmen's warnings about the dangerous temptation to go easy on what she called "subbies," or submissive males. "Don't do it! Next thing you know, they're sitting on the furniture and reaching for the TV remote. Once you've got them down, you've got to step on them hard and keep them down."

Of course, that's exactly what Kelly had done to Chris when she'd come home tonight, literally grinding his face into the rug with her bare foot. But she decided it would be fun to torment him a bit more by telling him about Henry Malcolm.

"Anyway, that's ancient history. I chose you, because, well, even if he was a specimen, he was, frankly, kind of a lug. No, when I say a real man, I'm thinking of someone I met on this last sales trip. Did I ever mention Henry Malcolm to you?"

"No, Goddess."

"Well, it's probably time I did. He's terribly attractive. An older man, mid-fifties, I'd guess. Does that surprise you, that I could be attracted to an older man?"

"No, Goddess, it doesn't."

"He even has white hair, which goes wonderfully with his rugged tan. Henry's an outdoorsman. Hunter, fisherman, yachtsman, you name it. He builds things. Golf courses, resorts, even airports, all over the world.

"He grew up in South Africa, actually spent time in his teens living with some local tribes and later wrote a book about it. He told me that among the Masai, a boy becomes a man only after killing his first lion. You know, one of those rite-of-passage thingies. Henry actually did that when he was nineteen, with a fucking spear, can you imagine? Have you ever speared a lion, sweetie? Hmm? No? I didn't think so. Maybe that's why you'll never be a real man, why I can't help turning you into my little lapdog and whipping boy. Isn't that about right?"

She reached out and slapped his now-erect shaft, sending it on a comical, side-to-side wobble. Except for a quick wince of pain, Chris suffered this humiliation in silence.

"Well? Am I right in what I just said about you?"

"Yes, Goddess, you are."

"You don't disagree with me on anything, do you, little slave? You don't dare." And, with a derisive snort, Kelly slapped his cock sideways again. "Which rather makes my point, doesn't it? Henry Malcolm is everything you're not, Slaveboy. He swaggers, while you grovel. I couldn't tame Henry if I tried, and, believe me, I have no intention of trying. I like him just the way he is. Want to hear how we met?"

"No!" Christopher wanted to shout. Instead, groaning inwardly, he merely nodded, knowing she was going to tell him anyway.

"It was a week ago today, up in BC..." The initials meant British Columbia, Chris knew, where Kelly's company owned several resorts. Malcolm Global, Henry's construction firm, she explained, was rebuilding a resort hotel in the Bugaboo Mountains and expanding its golf course from nine to eighteen holes. He'd taken her around in his

Jeep to view the work in progress. It was at the final panoramic overlook, as he'd swung around from describing what the bulldozers were creating, that their faces ended up only inches apart—and he'd kissed her.

"And you—you let him?" Unable to stop himself, Chris had blurted out the impertinent question.

"*Let* him? My God, Chris, I absolutely melted in his arms! I felt like Scarlett O'Hara being French-kissed by Rhett Butler! My heart went pitter-patter, and, believe me, that wasn't the only part of me that responded." Playfully, Kelly mimed fanning herself like a Southern Belle having a fit of the vapors.

"What about your rule about clients and—"

"Did I say he was a client? Well, actually, he turned out to be one. Besides being the CEO of Malcolm Global, Henry represents an industry association of golf course builders, and I was up there hustling their convention business. But, alas, you're right, sweetie. I do have that nasty old rule, and I can't tell you how many times it's spoiled my fun. I came awfully close to breaking it with Henry, though. We spent some quality time up there on that overlook, I'll tell you. I got a contract out of it, but poor Henry didn't get what he wanted, not all of it anyway."

"So, so—then you didn't, uh—actually—"

"Fuck him? No, not yet, sweetie. We've been texting back and forth ever since, though, like a couple of hormone-crazed high school kids."

Chris was hit by yet another spasm of impotent jealousy. He was forbidden to text Kelly during work hours, except in an emergency, and here she was texting back and forth with some old bastard who couldn't wait to cuckold him.

"What—what's going to happen next?"

"Whatever happens or doesn't happen, it's none of your business—unless I choose to tell you. And that's always been the case, hasn't it, Christopher? As I explicitly told you when we got married, ours was not and never would be a marriage of equals. I have absolute freedom. While you—well, you live under my absolute control, don't you? I mean, like keeping you naked. It's convenient for me to be able to touch you anywhere and at any time," and here she snapped a finger against the tip of his penis, causing him to yelp and rise up on his toes. "But you've always been totally available to me, while you dare not touch your Goddess without express permission.

"And there are my orgasms. It's your duty to help me achieve an unlimited number, while you're denied for weeks or months at a time. Sex, in other words, has always been exclusively for my benefit and pleasure, not yours.

"But somehow you've forgotten your place. Maybe because I took you home to meet my parents and dressed you up like a real groom, you got carried away and started imagining you were a real husband, and that I actually belong to you in some witless way, just like all the other Neanderthals who think they own their wives.

"And, frankly, I've let you get away with your delusion. Because I've been working too incredibly hard to even think about outside sex, let alone pursue it. And whenever I need to take the edge off, you're always handy." And here she took him in hand again. "Sort of like my bedside vibrator, only with an extra-special clit-licking tongue attachment. So, sweetie, you've lucked into a kind of sexual exclusivity by default. And it's given you ridiculous notions about exactly who and what you are.

"But all that's going to end. Do you know what some dominant mistresses do to their slaves to teach them their place?"

"Well, I've seen some weird stuff on the 'net."

"I know you have, but that's over, too. You just got permanently logged off. Anyway, I'm not talking about Internet fantasy sites, but about real-life female supremacists who actually own male slaves. I'm close friends with one now, and I've learned a lot from her about the lifestyle. Some dommes she knows keep their males locked up in cages. Others keep them shackled, with a long heavy chain that is tethered to some central point so the slave can still do all his housework, dragging his chain from room to room.

"Imagine what that would feel like, Christopher, dragging a chain behind you like Marley's Ghost with every step. Would you be able to forget, even for one second, that you were the property of a superior female?"

"No, Goddess, I wouldn't."

"No, you certainly wouldn't! So, tell me, would you like it if I did that to you? Something tells me that you would."

The "something," of course, was his penis, still cradled in her palm, which had been visibly writhing and enlarging throughout her little recitation of cruelties, and was now actually leaking precum.

"My, my, Christopher! All this seems to be getting you more and more excited! Why do you suppose that is?"

"I don't know, Goddess." And, really, he didn't. All he knew was that it did, God help him.

"So let's be clear about this, sweetie. If I got you a dog cage, and snapped my finger and pointed inside, you'd crawl right into it, wouldn't you?"

"Yes, Goddess," he heard himself say feebly.

"And what if I wanted to fasten a leg iron around your ankle, so I could chain you up? Would you sit perfectly still while I did it?"

"Yes, Goddess."

"Excellent! Now, tell me, please, do you think those are the answers that a man, a real man like, say, Henry Malcolm, would give?"

"No, Goddess."

"No, they're not. But they're the right answers for my pathetic little worm, aren't they?"

"Yes, Goddess."

"Well, if you're very, very good, sweetie, or very, very bad, perhaps your perverted little dreams will come true one day soon. But for right now, I have a little something to help you get started on your new life. A special present. Do you want to see it?"

"Yes, Goddess." He felt his pulse quicken with submissive anticipation.

"Then go fetch my briefcase by the front door."

Chris turned to obey, but she snapped at him: "What do you think you're doing, slave?"

"Going to fetch your briefcase, Goddess."

"Did I say you could walk?"

"No, Goddess. I just thought—"

"Don't think!" Kelly slapped his face hard and pointed to the floor. "Just remember your place!"

Chris dropped to all fours and scooted away, ball sac swinging between his thighs. Kelly, meanwhile, had leaned back and closed her eyes, fingering her sex again. Erotic images were swarming anew in her brain, images of Christopher bent over the loveseat, naked and defenseless, awaiting that first cruel kiss of her heavy strap.

What was it Carmen had said about this stuff being addictive? It

108

had been less than an hour, and already Kelly couldn't wait for next time!

When she opened her eyes, she saw her slave kneeling before her, head down, presenting the briefcase in outstretched hands.

Kelly took it and thumbed open the brass catches, then lifted out a gift-wrapped package the approximate size and shape of a Kleenex cube box.

She handed it to Christopher. "For you, sweetie. Open it."

Chris stared at the little box with both dread and excitement. By now he had a pretty good idea of what was inside.

"Isn't the wrapping absolutely darling!"

"Uh-huh," Chris said. It was done up in white tissue paper crisscrossed with pink satin ribbon with a curlicue bow.

He undid the girlie wrapping carefully, lest he be scolded or slapped for tearing anything, then pried open the cardboard box and looked inside.

CHAPTER TWELVE ~ A SPECIAL PRESENT ~ TWO

Inside the box Christopher found exactly what he'd expected—a male chastity device.

He stared in horrid fascination. This wasn't a molded tube of clear plastic or silicone, like most he'd seen on x-rated Internet sites. It was a shiny spiral of stainless steel, almost like a mini-shock absorber, but with a penile droop that made its function explicit. It was a metal cage to lock up his manhood—for as long as Kelly wanted.

And comparing its modest size to his now swollen penis made it starkly obvious that, once inside, he could never get hard again.

"Go on, sweetie, take it out of the box. It won't bite you."

"Yes, Goddess." Chris did as told. Inside the box, in addition to the stainless coil, there was a small, stainless steel ring and a tiny brass padlock with two keys. He handed everything over to Kelly.

"I take it you have a pretty good idea what this is?"

"Yes, Goddess, I do."

"Are you ready, then, brave boy?"

He nodded.

"So let's get it on you. We do have a slight problem, though." She grasped his engorged shaft and tugged him closer. "You're not very big, as I've said, but even so, we can't fit you inside until we shrink you back to normal. What do you suggest, sweetie? And no, I'm not going to let you shoot off for a last hurrah, so don't even beg."

"I won't, Goddess."

"The quickest solution, of course, is the way I did it before.

Remember?" Kelly closed her fist purposefully around his scrotum, noting with satisfaction his involuntary flinch of fear. "Or we can simply use ice cubes. Your choice, Slaveboy."

"Ice cubes, please, Goddess."

And so, a moment later, Chris was back on hands and knees, his entire backside still aflame as he crawled naked over the cold kitchen floor tiles. And, for an indelible second, he got an out-of-body flash of himself as he would look to any normal male right now—to a macho guy like that South African bastard, or, much worse, to his own father, a tough-talking electrician who'd learned his trade in the Navy.

"Goddammit, Chris, stand up like a man!" he could hear the Old Man bellowing in disgust. "What the hell's wrong with you? You never let a woman—"

But Chris did not stand up. In fact, he found within himself not the slightest resistance to Kelly's absolute rule. Ironic, only yesterday he had vowed there was no way he'd ever let her put a cock lock on him. And now here he was, in total, submissive freefall, eager to surrender the last bastion of his manhood.

Following her slightly amended instructions, he opened the freezer door and fished out a bag of frozen peas, then crawled obediently back to her with the bag clamped in his teeth.

Kelly watched him coming, feeling incredibly sexy and powerful at seeing her cute little hubby stripped of clothes and dignity, reduced to the status of her trained puppy. But if Chris imagined he was being treated harshly, he was mistaken. He had no idea that he was being let off easily.

During her stopover at Carmen's apartment on the way home, Kelly had witnessed a far more brutally efficient method for subduing a slave's erection. Carmen had had Hector stand before them, head bowed, his cartoonishly muscled and tattooed body stark naked except for his own spiral cock cage.

In fact, Kelly was startled to discover on close inspection, the Latino's nakedness included a total absence of pubic hair.

"My God, Carmen, do you shave him?"

"Fuck no! I make him do it himself, every day, and his scrotum and ass cheeks, too. It helps him remember he's not a real man anymore, just my little toyboy. Maybe you should try it on Chris."

"Maybe I will."

"Now watch closely." Carmen unlocked Hector's chastity device with a tiny key she kept on a gold chain around her neck. Once liberated, his penis had sprung straight up, rock hard.

"Okay, I'm properly impressed!" Kelly said.

"Is he bigger than your Chris?"

"Definitely! A lot thicker, probably longer, too." Which was remarkable, Kelly thought, since Hector looked to be only five-eight or -nine, while Christopher was almost six feet tall.

"That'll work out great then!" Carmen had said.

"Sure! For you, not for me. I like big cocks, too."

"That's not what I mean. The thing is, if your guy's smaller, maybe he can fit into Hector's old model, which has an inside diameter about a half-inch smaller than this one. Hec kept whining and complaining till I got him a bigger tube, and now he's a happy little subbie, aren't you, baby?"

"Yes, Mistress." Hector kept his eyes downcast.

"I'll get his old one for you in a moment. But right now let me show you how I stuff him back inside."

With her riding crop, Carmen gave Hector several hard lashes across his muscular buttocks. Though the bodybuilder had grunted at each blow in obvious pain, he had maintained his erection.

"Now your turn." Carmen passed the leather crop to Kelly. "But not on his butt. Give him a good whack right in the *huevos.*"

"You're not serious?"

"Of course I'm serious! He's just a slave. He has to take whatever you dish out."

"How hard?"

"As hard as you can. Pretend they're two tiny *piñatas* and you want to spill out all the candy inside."

Hector had remained silent during this exchange, head down, cock still proudly rampant. But Kelly saw his nostrils flare and his abdominals tighten in anticipation.

Her well-aimed blow had sent him groaning to his knees and shriveled his erection. The effect on Kelly had been even more dramatic, though less visible. It had reminded her of the cocaine rush she'd gotten at that yacht party in Nassau Harbor. Except that first and only experience of the mind-altering drug had scared hell out of her, while flogging the private parts of this defenseless male had left her definitely wanting more.

When the muscular Latino was able to stand before them again, head still cowed, Carmen had insisted that Kelly do the honors of putting him back into chastity. Kelly had giggled at first, but carefully completed the simple procedure to Carmen's satisfaction before Hector was dismissed to his designated corner.

Now, lacking a riding crop of her own, Kelly made do with the frozen peas, ignoring Christopher's sudden gasps as she bent the icy bag around the base of his shaft. In no time at all his penis had shrunk sufficiently so she could insert it through the base ring along with his balls, one at a time, mindful of Carmen's admonition:

"You don't have to handle them like they're the fucking crown jewels! Just shove 'em through."

Next she inserted Chris' wilted member into the steel cage, working it forward with her fingers through the spiral coils; then joining the cage to the base ring with the small locking pin; and, a second later, securing the assembled device with a click of the tiny brass padlock.

"*Voilà!*" she said, setting the keys on the side table. "You are now officially my property and chattel. How do you like it? Does it make you feel very special, slave?"

"Yes, Goddess, it does."

Chris looked down, feeling both defeated and proud at the same time. In fact, the excitement of being Kelly's padlocked property was already swelling his penis again. He could feel it trying to expand against the cold steel ribs of his cage, felt the cage walls embracing him, and holding him downward.

"Look, poor little Johnny Wobble is trying to get out!"

It was true. Chris' penis was now pressed hard against the bars, forcing ridges of his skin up between the spirals of metal.

"Are you sure it's—it's the right size, Goddess?" Chris asked hesitantly.

"It has to be." Kelly chuckled. "It's the only one I've got! But, seriously, I checked, and it's definitely the right size. I'm afraid you're a 'small,' sweetie, not even a 'medium.'"

"Will I wear it always, Goddess?"

"You mean will I ever let you out? Hmm, I'll have to get back to you on that. The important thing for now is, we've finally found a permanent cure for your nasty little habit. You now join the ranks of inferior males who live under total female supervision. How does that feel?"

"It feels right, Goddess. I—I want to be your property."

"Oh, my God, are you tearing up again? Are we going to have more crying, little slave?"

"No, Goddess." But this solemn promise was being broken even as it was made. Chris dropped to his knees, embraced her calves and lay his head in her lap, sobbing pitifully. Kelly sighed and patted his curly head, saying soft and meaningless words.

Her mind, however, was a million miles away, caught up in a swirl of erotic possibilities. Some of her vivid imaginings were inspired by Carmen, some were of her own devising. And yet others had nothing at all to do with Christopher, except insofar as his complete subjugation now freed her to explore various aspects of her sexual supremacy.

When, after a very few minutes, Kelly became annoyed with all his clutching and crying, she slapped him and sent him off to bed—or, rather to her sleeping bag, giving him instructions to roll it out at the foot of her bed.

Fifteen minutes later, after bringing him some warm milk and letting him briefly kiss the bottom of her bare foot, she finally closed the door on her slave. It was a great relief, back in her recliner, to savor a long taste of Malbec and a hot forkful of a petite quiche just out of the microwave.

On the side table, for dessert, was another item on loan from Carmen, a DVD entitled "The Governess' Male Discipline Training, Series 2." And right beside it was her favorite vibrating wand.

Altogether a satisfying end to a satisfying day.

CHAPTER THIRTEEN ~ HIS NEW LIFE

For Christopher, on that first morning of his new life, everything was strange. Like a drunk emerging from a monumental bender, he began, carefully and cautiously, to piece together all the lurid scraps of memory, hoping to fit them into some kind of coherence.

Her foot was on his face. He had kissed that foot, both of her perfect feet, kissed them and shed tears on them. He had been slapped, many times, scolded and laughed at. His balls had been crushed in her hand. He had been stood in a corner for endless, excruciating minutes, forced to keep a penny trapped against the wall with the tip of his nose. But afterward she had opened her blouse and fed him her magnificent tit...

He relived the perfect happiness of that moment, but the memory was swept away by the Other Thing, the thing that explained the shameful nexus of pain all down his back and buttocks and legs.

He'd been beaten, like an animal is beaten. He heard and felt again in memory the merciless explosions of leather against his burning flesh. He had suffered the terrible wrath of Goddess Juno herself. He had suffered—and survived.

But not intact. Because the beating had taken something from him, something precious and irreplaceable, something he would never get back.

"You are not a man anymore." He spoke the words aloud, slowly and softly, knowing them to contain profound and terrible truth. "She took that away from you."

How fitting, then, that he'd spent the night here on the floor, at the foot of her bed, a place where a dog would sleep, and not in her bed like a man.

Never again in her bed.

Chris worked his right hand down inside the sleeping bag to feel the cold metal of the spiral cage she'd locked on him. The cage that kept him from touching himself, that even now prevented his penis from reaching its morning fullness.

A man would feel outrage at this ultimate indignity. Chris was filled with twisted pride.

"This is your new life, slave."

Those were the final words she'd said to him last night—her voice husky, incredibly sexy and all-powerful—just before she'd closed the door and left him alone in the darkness…

THE END of Part One.
"Chapter Thirteen" continues, and the adventure concludes, in *Dancing Backward 2: A Final Descent Into Male Submission.*

ALSO AVAILABLE FROM THOMAS LAVALLE:

DANCING BACKWARD 2:
FINAL DESCENT INTO MALE SUBMISSION

DANCING BACKWARD 2 takes up this most unconventional love story where Book One left off— on the night of Christopher's shocking and mind-blowing initiation into what seems total submission to his ravishing ruling wife, whom he now addresses and worships as Goddess Kelly. But, as he will quickly discover, many additional initiations and levels await in his downward journey into total subjugation. All of them are delightfully detailed in this 70,000-word sequel that plumbs the psychoerotic and spiritual depths of Female Supremacy.

A few of the Amazon 5-star reviews for Dancing Backward 2:
- "Great femdom story – one I couldn't stop reading!"
- "Terrific continuation of Kelly and Chris' saga. Please keep producing, Thomas!"
- "A compelling femdom novel!"

The three-part femdom epic concludes with:
DANCING BACKWARD 3:
A BELOVED SLAVE RECLAIMED

The 90,000-word finale of the three-part femdom epic, featuring the concluding misadventures of Christopher and Goddess Kelly. These include a series of harrowing escapes and recaptures, provocative glimpses into strict female-led families and secret gynarchic societies—and the surprise ending of this most unusual love story.

Made in the USA
Columbia, SC
25 September 2021

46169222R00076